"I chose you for a reason, Kara. You're just the kind of woman I'm after."

"And what kind of woman is that?"

Matt placed his fingertips together, leaned his elbows on the table and stared directly into her eyes. "Smart, independent, with no romantic illusions. You're the perfect choice for me."

Confusion whirled through her mind. "I don't get it."

"I'm looking for a business arrangement. Nothing more. You will appear as my steady girlfriend for the next six months, till I secure a partnership in Dad's firm. That's it."

Nicola Marsh says, "As a girl, I dreamed of being a journalist and traveling the world in search of the next big story. Luckily, I have had the opportunity to travel the world, but my dream to write has never been far from my mind. When I met my own tall, dark and handsome hero, and learned that romance *is* everything it's cracked up to be, I finally took the plunge and put pen to paper. I live in the southeastern suburbs of Melbourne with my husband and a baby. When I'm not writing, I work as a physiotherapist for a vocational rehabilitation company, helping people with disabilities return to the workforce. I also love sharing fine food and wine with friends and family, going to the movies and, my favorite, curling up in front of the fire with a good book."

This is Nicola's first book!

THE TYCOON'S DATING DEAL

Nicola Marsh

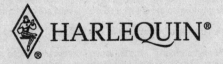

HARLEQUIN®

TORONTO • NEW YORK • LONDON
AMSTERDAM • PARIS • SYDNEY • HAMBURG
STOCKHOLM • ATHENS • TOKYO • MILAN • MADRID
PRAGUE • WARSAW • BUDAPEST • AUCKLAND

To Mum and Dad, for a lifetime of love,
and to Martin, for believing in me and our dream

ISBN 0-373-03810-0

THE TYCOON'S DATING DEAL

First North American Publication 2004.

Copyright © 2004 by Nicola Marsh.

This edition published by arrangement with Harlequin Books S.A.

www.eHarlequin.com

Printed in U.S.A.

CHAPTER ONE

'YOU want me to do *what*?'

Kara Roberts stared at her best friend in disbelief. As much as she loved Sally, this time she had gone too far.

'Please, Kara. Pretty please. You know my butt's on the line, not to mention my business,' Sally cajoled, a hint of fear in her eyes.

Kara knew she was beaten. She had never seen Sally so desperate. The agency must be in more trouble than the older woman had let on.

Flopping into a nearby chair, Kara folded her arms and leaned back. 'OK, I'll do it. Though just this once. You owe me big time, Sal. Real big.'

Sally flew across the room, her greying curls bouncing around her chubby face, and enveloped her in a bear hug.

'Thanks, sweetie. You're one in a million.'

Tears glittered in Sally's brown eyes as she pulled away. Kara's heart swelled with love for the amazing woman who had taken her in, without question, following her parents' death. She'd been twelve years old when the two most important people in her life had died in a car accident. Sally, her mum's best friend, had stepped in and offered her a home. Not just a home. She had supported, encouraged and loved her throughout the difficult teenage years and beyond.

This one favour for Sally, tricky as it may be, would be small repayment for years of love and friendship.

'OK, now that my neck is on the line, what do I do?'

Sally shuffled through the mountain of paperwork on her desk. 'Here. Fill these out for a start. This has to be legit, so complete every form and sign on the dotted line.'

Kara took the stack of forms and leafed through them, seeing but not quite believing what she was reading. 'You've got to be kidding, Sal. Eye colour of desired partner? Most romantic dinner? Most erotic place to be kissed? Where do you get this stuff?'

Sally crossed her arms, puffed out her cheeks and slowly exhaled. 'I need that info to process your data into the computer. You know that. You've laughed about it for years, not to mention seen how it works. Why the cold feet now?'

Kara chuckled. 'I've laughed about it when these ridiculous questions are applied to other people. Now that I'm under the microscope, it's not so funny.

Besides, can't I just skip this part and get the dating over and done with?'

Sally shook her head. 'If I'm to win the award for Sydney's Dating Agency of the Year, I need you to complete everything. Your application will be processed with the rest of the applicants. Kara, I wouldn't ask you to do this if I weren't desperate. When Maggie pulled out this morning, I was floundering. All you need to do is attend the speed-dating dinner tonight.'

'Hah! Easy for you to say. What if someone I know sees me? They'll think I'm some kind of desperado.'

Hurt flickered in Sally's eyes. Matchmaker meant the world to her. Her own business was precious, so why should Sally's be any different?

'Like the rest of my clients, you mean?' Sally asked.

'Sorry, Sal. I'm just not used to all this. I prefer to get my dates the usual way.'

Sally's eyebrows shot heavenward. 'Which way is that? You haven't had a date in over a year!'

How the truth hurt. She'd steered clear of men over the last twelve months, tired of their game-playing. Most of her dates were only after one thing and she was sick of the whole scene.

'That's a bit harsh. I've had plenty of dates in the last few years.' She ignored the empty feeling that arose whenever the subject of men entered a conversation. Only one man had ever made her feel special and he was gone. Long gone.

'Sure you have, sweetie, which is why you spend most of your free time with an old chook like me.'

'You, old? Sure, there may be a few greys sprinkled in your hair and a couple of laughter-lines around your eyes, but old? Is that why you prefer to screen the male candidates personally? You forget, I've seen the way you glow after a session with some of your hunky applicants.'

Her teasing fell on deaf ears as Sally rustled the papers in front of her, suddenly businesslike.

'Thanks for the confidence boost. You forgot to mention the extra forty pounds I'm carrying at the moment. Anyway, enough small talk. Complete these forms, missy, as I need to process them immediately. Then I think you'd better head home and get ready. I've got one last male to meet today and then tonight is all set. Once I've matched my thousandth couple, the DATY award has to be mine.'

Kara barely glanced at the forms, her stomach churning at the worried look on Sally's face.

'Is the agency in that much trouble, Sal?'

Though her own funds were limited since Inner Sanctum, her interior-design business, had drained most of her money, she would take a loan if needed to help Sally.

'If I don't win the DATY, Matchmaker will have to shut up shop. The prize money would go a long way to updating the computer system and the prestige will put this agency on the map.' Sally sighed. 'So yeah, you could say I'm in trouble.'

'But how?' Kara probed, knowing she wouldn't like the answer. Guilt consumed her, increasing the tumultuous turning of her gut. In fact, she had a fair idea of what Sally was about to say.

'I've never been a rich woman, darling, you know that. I put everything into making a home for us, with my investments providing the money to start up this.' She threw her arms wide, indicating the office that served as Matchmaker's headquarters. 'I guess I didn't do my sums right.'

Kara knew there was more to it than that. What Sally hadn't mentioned was the amount of money she had loaned her to start Inner Sanctum.

Unable to ignore the overwhelming guilt any longer, she picked up the pen lying on Sally's desk and started filling out forms.

'If I can do anything else apart from this, Sal, you let me know.'

'Just keep writing, love, and I'll take care of the rest.'

Within minutes, Kara had completed the forms. In several hours she would be having drinks with a bunch of strangers with the aim of finding a 'suitable' partner. If it weren't for the fact that Sally was desperate, she would tear up her application on the spot.

She'd been looking forward to going home, slipping into a hot bath and listening to the soothing sounds of her favourite soul singer. Today hadn't been one of her better days. The Smithsons, who owned half of exclusive Double Bay, had been pestering her to redesign their conservatory. Unfortunately, she'd had to endure the wailing violin practice from their prodigy granddaughter for the entire two hours that it took to discuss the plans.

Sally's call on her mobile phone had been welcome. Momentarily. In fact, in choosing between an evening of speed dating and spending another few hours with the screeching violin, Kara was wavering towards the violin.

'So I'll see you tonight?'

Kara sighed. 'Yeah, I suppose.'

Sally laughed. 'You've got that look. You know, the one you always had when I dragged you off to the dentist.'

'You're not far off the mark, Sal. The way I'm feeling at the moment, I think I'd rather have a tooth pulled.'

Sally patted her cheek, love radiating from her brown eyes. 'Why don't you head home and relax? The evening will be over before you know it.'

'Mmm,' she mumbled, already preoccupied with thoughts of making idle chit-chat with a bunch of strange men.

Shutting the door to Sally's inner office, she glanced around the reception area with pride. Not bad for a novice, she thought, considering the office had been one of her early projects. She loved her job, particularly the artistic licence of combining colours, shapes and dimensions in an imaginative free-for-all. A pity her customers didn't think the same; after a busy few months when she first opened, business had slowed to a crawl. Sal wasn't the only one who desperately needed money. Kara needed a cash injection—and fast.

As she reached for the outer door, it was flung open, almost knocking her sideways.

'Sorry. Are you OK?'

No, I'm not. She stared into the face of the last man she'd expected to see. Entering a dating agency, no less!

'Kara? What a surprise.'

Matthew Byrne's strong arms enveloped her in a vice-like hug. All the old feelings rushed back: longing and desire for the man, inadequacy at being the woman he didn't want. She hadn't mastered her emotions one iota. He still had the power to reduce her to a blathering idiot. Not that she would let him know.

'Hi, Matt. Good to see you.' She almost choked on the words as she eased from his embrace. Her head was spinning, her pulse racing. He'd probably restricted her oxygen supply, he'd hugged her so tight.

'Look at you, all grown up.'

As his gaze raked over her body, goosebumps peppered her skin. His stare lingered on her breasts a second too long before returning to her face.

She crossed her arms over her chest, trying to look casual yet knowing she failed miserably.

To her chagrin, he grinned, the same devilish smile that had haunted her dreams for years. He had seen her reaction and was probably loving every minute of it.

Lifting her chin, she glared at him.

'Yeah, that tends to happen to *little girls*.'

She wondered if he remembered those painful words he'd uttered on the night of her eighteenth birthday. The night he'd broken her heart.

A flicker of awareness leaped in the azure depths of his eyes before he masked it.

'Well, you're far from little any more. You look gorgeous. It's a shame we haven't stayed in touch over the years.'

Kara could drown in the endless blue of his eyes. She'd never seen a colour like them, that potent mix of violet and sapphire, with the barest hint of emerald. A corny way to describe them, yet nothing but flowery language could come close to describing their brilliance. Purple, blue and green would be far too ordinary for the likes of Matt Byrne's eyes.

·Her skin warmed as a slow blush crept into her cheeks. She could guess what it would have been like to 'keep in touch', Matt-style. His hands lightly caressing every inch of her skin, his lips trailing over her body, exploring her most intimate secrets.

As if sensing her thoughts, he reached towards her and cupped her cheek.

'You look adorable, blushing like that. Still the same old Kara, huh?'

His low, husky voice raspeu across her nerve endings. She yearned to lean into his hand, to feel the comfort that only he could give.

Instead, she remembered the crushing kiss, frantic hands and then the powerful rejection that had lasted a lifetime. Matt Byrne had pushed her away in the cruellest way possible, belittling her to the point where she couldn't speak to him again.

Now here he was, sauntering into her life like a superhero and acting the part: flexed muscles, broad chest, chiselled face, killer smile. All he needed was the cape and his underwear on the outside of his designer suit and the picture would be complete.

She laughed. The underwear image did it. Once

lodged in her brain, she couldn't stop thinking about it.

'What's so funny?' Matt's hundred-watt smile faltered.

'Sorry. Just old memories. You know how it is.' She wiped the tears from her eyes, hoping that her mascara hadn't smudged.

'I didn't think our memories were that funny.' He rubbed her upper arms, running his hands under the sleeves of her T-shirt. It was an intimate caress, one that frightened her with its power to arouse.

She pulled back before she did something really stupid, like stand there helpless and let him kiss her. Which was what he looked like doing, though she couldn't fathom why.

'All ancient history. I hear you've moved on to bigger and better things. Your life as the corporate-lawyer-cum-playboy must be filled with more excitement than old memories.'

His eyes narrowed, some of the light vanishing. 'Don't believe everything you read. The media thrive on gossip to sell their print.'

'Well, you must have shares, because your reported behaviour could sell a million copies alone.'

She sounded catty but couldn't help the annoyance at some of his antics, if the newspapers were correct.

Matt featured in the gossip columns on a weekly basis, an endless supply of beautiful, silicone-enhanced women draped over his arm. And other parts, no doubt. His reputation as a playboy was plastered all over the Sydney papers. She'd had a lucky escape. So why did she always screw up the newspaper in a tight ball and fling it across the room every time Matt Byrne and his latest *acquisition* were mentioned?

'Speaking of reputations, what are you doing here? You're the last man I'd expect to see waltzing into a dating agency. Problem with your charm?'

Though her teasing was light-hearted, she noticed his smile waned. Matt wasn't as cool as he pretended. She had struck a nerve.

His laugh sounded forced. 'Nothing wrong with my *charm,* Kara. You should know that.'

She could hardly disagree when he was standing right in front of her, resurrecting provocative memories that she'd successfully suppressed. Until now. 'So, why are you here?'

His reply was short, sharp and ominous. 'Business.' Damn, Sally must be in more trouble than she thought if lawyers were already on her tail.

'Go easy on her, won't you?' she said, wishing once again there was something else she could do for Sally.

She didn't understand the look that flashed across his face momentarily. His face was an intriguing combination of angles: smooth yet hard, straight yet curved. A faint stubble darkened his jaw, typical of his end-of-day growth. Lord, she'd give anything to feel that stubble rubbed along any part of her body. Or all of it for that matter!

'Kara? Are you OK? You look kind of flushed.'

Wrenching her attention back to the present, Kara knew she had to escape. Now. He still held a strange, hypnotic power over her. She'd always been prone to fantasies around him and it looked as though nothing had changed. In nine long years she hadn't mastered her feelings where he was concerned. The knowledge was scary.

The years and countless dates since had done little to erase the image of this man from her mind. He was imprinted on her mind and soul, seemingly forever.

Definitely scary.

Given the fight or flight option, she chose the latter.

'Yes, I'm fine, Matt. Great seeing you again. Hope whatever you're here for works out.'

She hesitated, memorising every detail of his face. *Old habits die hard.*

'Thanks; nice seeing you too. Perhaps we'll catch up for a drink one day soon?'

She ignored her thudding heart. 'I don't think so. Thanks anyway. Bye.'

She rushed out the door before he could respond.

Don't look back. He'll think you're still hung up on him.

She'd never been any good at listening to reason and risked a quick glance over her shoulder. He stared at her through the window. Funnily enough, he stood directly under the sign 'Matchmaker', which was emblazoned on the glass in red lettering. No chance of that ever happening. Matt Byrne, playboy extraordinaire, finding his perfect match and settling down? Not a hope in hell.

Matt stared at Kara's back and tried to ignore the erotic images that filtered through his brain. She'd grown up. And then some. The statuesque strawberry blonde was all hot curves and big green eyes now. Not to mention everything else. Wow!

He was used to beautiful women. His world was inundated with them. Intelligent, gorgeous women who were more than eager to spend some time with him: lawyers, accountants, stockbrokers. The list was endless. However, none had captured his attention in a long time. Until Kara. She was a stunner, from her cat-like eyes to her shiny, reddish-blonde hair that hung in a sleek curtain down her back.

She'd been a nice-looking kid who had blossomed around the age of sixteen. He still remembered their endless talks, the sharing of confidences, the easy friendship...then Kara had grown up. Almost overnight his hormones had shifted into overdrive and all he could think of every waking moment, and most dreaming ones too, was Kara.

He'd wanted her with a fierceness that had scared him. He should have known better, being older, wiser, like a big brother to her. Even now, years later, he couldn't forget the innocent passion of her kiss as she had flung herself at him on her eighteenth birthday. For one brief moment Matt had lost himself, all his fantasies come true, until he realised who he was kissing. He'd overreacted, pushing her away with an icy, verbal barrage that would have doused the hottest flames.

After all, he hadn't wanted history repeating itself. One cradle-snatching Byrne in the family was enough and look how that had turned out. He could kill his dad sometimes, he really could.

He'd done the only decent thing possible and avoided Kara like the plague. Until today. Damn, he still had it bad. She was hotter than hot. He thought she'd shown some interest in return, then she'd bolted.

No harm in catching up over drinks, surely?

Yeah, right. She probably remembered the way he'd treated her all those years ago. No wonder she wouldn't have a drink with him.

And why the hell had she been in a dating agency? A woman like her wouldn't be single for long. What *he* wouldn't give to spend some time alone with her now.

Thrusting away his wayward thoughts, he rang the bell on the front counter.

'Be with you in a minute,' a voice shouted from the back office.

Matt glanced around, the ever-observant lawyer in him coming to the fore. The office was perfectly co-ordinated in black and chrome with the occasional splash of red to brighten it. No tacky hearts plastering the walls of this dating agency, just trendy stencilled prints by some artist he hadn't heard of. Not that he was an expert on dating agencies. This was the first he had been to and he hoped to God it would be the last.

'Sorry to keep you waiting.'

He turned, thinking the woman's voice sounded strangely familiar.

'Sally? Damn, this day just gets stranger and stranger. First Kara and now you.'

The older woman hugged him. 'Great to see you, Matt. You're as handsome as ever.'

She picked at imaginary loose threads on his suit jacket, bringing back treasured memories of his first ball, when Sally had stood proudly on his parent's doorstep and waved him off as if he were her child. In fact, she'd been more of a parent to him than his own father.

'You're looking great too, Sally.' He smiled, watching her already ruddy cheeks blush.

'Get away with you!' She slapped his arm playfully. 'So what brings you to Matchmaker? I wouldn't think you'd need much help in that department.'

'You run this agency?'

Relief washed over him. If Sally ran the agency, Kara had been visiting her surrogate mum rather than organising a date.

She nodded. 'Sure do. Opened it a few years ago, once Kara moved out and started her own business. I'd always had a smidgeon of an idea that I'd like to bring joy to lonely people, so after watching too much Oprah and reading too many romance novels, I decided to take the plunge.'

'That's great.' He thought about asking Sally about Kara's business but knew it was too obvious. Besides, he had plenty of time to do that. 'I need your help.'

'Come in, take a seat and tell old Sal all about it.'

He followed her into a small but equally appealing office. The tones were similar to the outer office, but lighter, giving the room an appearance of more space.

'So, handsome? Spill the beans.'

He leaned back in the comfortable chair and crossed his legs at the ankles.

'I need a change of image. My father thinks that my reputation is detrimental to the company.'

'Yeah, I see your antics plastered over the newspapers on a regular basis. You're quite the ladies' man.'

He shook his head. 'Don't believe everything you read. My life isn't half as exciting as the journalists make out. Anyway, Dad says I won't get a look-in at a partnership till my behaviour improves.'

He ran his hand through his hair, a habit he'd tried to conquer but failed, except in the courtroom.

'You know Dad. Byrne and Associates is his baby. I haven't a hope in Hades of making partner until I show "a more responsible attitude in my personal life", end of quote.'

Sally sighed. 'I was your dad's neighbour for a long time. He's very proud of you. Aren't you putting undue pressure on yourself here? He loves you, regardless of whether you make partner or not.'

Love? His father didn't know the meaning of the word. He straightened the knife-edge crease on his trousers. 'I need to prove to everyone at the firm that I'm a damn good lawyer who isn't just hanging onto Daddy's coat-tails. I want that partnership, the sooner the better.'

His blood pressure soared whenever he thought about the endless innuendos at the firm about his rising status in the company. He was a first-rate lawyer without the help of his father. Not that his dad had offered any.

'So, how can I help?'

This was the tricky part. Matt was embarrassed at having to admit that he'd already dated most of the women in his circle and beyond, and had found them lacking.

'Like I said, I need a change of image. I need to meet a woman, quickly, who is attuned to my way of thinking. I had a business arrangement in mind, where she would appear as my steady girlfriend for corporate events and the like. In return, she could name her price.'

Sally winced. 'Ouch! You make it sound so cold and calculating. I'm in the romance business, not in dating contracts. Besides, aren't you deceiving your father into offering you a partnership? Isn't there another way?'

He shook his head. 'I've done my research. Speed dating is the quickest and easiest way to meet a woman who matches my needs. I know the service is confidential so Dad won't find out. Besides, who is he to judge? Look at his personal life.'

'I still think it isn't right, you not telling your dad.'

Sally had always stuck up for his dad, though he couldn't for the life of him work out why. Jeff Byrne had been a cold-hearted father at times but Sally defended him, saying it was hard being a parent.

Problem was, his dad wouldn't know the first thing about being a parent, full stop.

'I want to do this, Sally. ASAP.'

There, he'd laid his cards on the table and she hadn't laughed at him.

A mischievous gleam shone from Sally's dark eyes. 'OK, enough of my lectures. Just fill out these forms and I'll lodge your data into the computer in a jiffy. After that, it's all systems go. You just turn up at the Blue Lounge tonight at eight and I'll be there to explain how everything works. Any questions?'

He wondered what the funny look on Sal's face was about. However, he'd come this far and decided to push his luck.

'Yeah, I have one. How can I contact Kara?'

Sally laughed and waggled a plump finger at him.

'That's all taken care of, my boy, and it's going to be sooner than you think.'

CHAPTER TWO

KARA strode into the Blue Lounge just before eight. A stickler for punctuality, she had deliberately driven a few laps around the block to kill time, not wanting to appear too eager. Thank goodness she was only doing this to help Sal and was not emotionally involved, unlike the rest of the patrons who were here to find their one true love. As far as she was concerned, she would do her duty, head home and leave the romance stuff to the lovelorn.

She scanned the dimly lit room, noting the intimate tables for two scattered around the perimeter. Her pulse quickened in apprehension at the thought of spending seven minutes with seven different men tonight. The tables were small enough to create a cosy ambience for their occupants. Rather than feigning indifference, she would be forced to make polite small talk before making a quick exit. Damn, she was anxious and hoped it didn't show.

She'd dressed to kill tonight: little black dress, silky stockings, strappy sequinned sandals and matching handbag. With just a hint of make-up to emphasise her eyes and lips and her hair twisted in

24

a stylish chignon, Kara knew she could pass any test. Pity the image hid a quivering mess of nerves inside.

She spotted Sally as soon as she sat down and smiled as Sally squeezed through the tables, beaming and waving at everyone like the Queen. Sally was a regular here, using this venue for her weekly gatherings.

'Hi, sweetie. You look sensational!'

Kara shrugged. 'What? This old thing?'

'I know you, my dear. Glam outfit and make-up, too? Your nerves must be working overtime!'

'Whatever gave you that idea?'

They laughed in unison. Sally knew Kara preferred understated elegance rather than knock 'em dead outfits, so it was òbvious she was nervous as hell.

'Never mind. You won't have time to be worried once the action starts. Now, you remember the rules?'

'Sal, don't fuss. I've known the rules for years. Who else listened to your ramblings about the agency, huh?'

Sally tweaked her nose, a toothy grin on her face. 'You encouraged me into this venture and don't you forget it.'

'Ow!' Kara rubbed her nose in mock pain. 'That was before I knew you'd turn your matchmaking skills on to me. Who knows what losers I'll end up wasting my time with tonight?'

Sally's grin widened. 'Oh, I wouldn't be too concerned if I were you. My computer has a happy knack of delivering just what a woman wants. It has a great track record, eight marriages in two years. Who knows, you might meet the man of your dreams? Then you'll be thanking old Sal rather than berating her.'

'Come off it. I don't need a man. I've got my business to run. I don't have time for anything or anyone else right now. And as for finding the man of my dreams, I'd have a better chance of winning the lottery.'

Sally's dark eyes twinkled. 'Oh, well, don't say I didn't warn you. Regardless of what happens tonight, thanks for helping me out, dear.'

Kara felt a twinge of guilt. The least she could do was act enthused. After all, the agency was Sal's pride and joy. If anyone could understand, she should. Her own business was floundering and she would do anything to save it.

She hugged the older woman. 'Everything will be fine, Sal. You'll match your thousandth couple tonight and the agency will kick on for the next ten years. Just mark my words. I'm glad I could help. What else are daughters for?'

Sally touched her cheek and sashayed away, her ample bottom draped in gold crêpe.

Kara missed her parents, though the agonising pain

of loss had dulled with time. Sally had seen to that, smothering her with love and attention, enveloping her in warmth and security. However, she would never forget those endless, empty nights, when she'd cried herself to sleep.

Matt had been supportive too. He'd listened to her tales of woe, teasing her, helping her with her homework. She'd been devastated when he'd left for university, only seeing him during the holidays.

However, when he returned home on holiday that first year, something had changed. Their open relationship became fraught with a tangible tension. She knew it had been her fault, as she'd developed a huge crush on Matt around this time. She'd tried to hide it but he obviously knew, because he'd treated her with kid gloves that summer and beyond. No more playful tickles or impulsive hugs. The object of her affection had kept his distance, driving her insane in the process.

Kara had followed suit until her eighteenth birthday. The memory of his rejection still turned her stomach. Yet today, when he'd appeared out of the blue, she'd almost swooned. No accounting for hormones.

'Excuse me. Is this seat taken?' A deep voice intruded on her memories.

'Actually, I'm waiting for…' Kara stared, momentarily speechless.

'This must be my lucky day. Seeing you twice in the space of a few hours... What are the odds of that happening?'

She looked at Matt's striking face, drinking in every detail: the laughter-lines at the outer corners of his eyes, the creases around his mouth, the dark shadow of stubble along his jaw line. Lord, he looked good. Her heart galloped, desire snaking through her body.

She clenched her hands under the table, willing her mind and mouth to work in synchronisation. 'I don't know, Matt. You tell me—you're the gambling man...if your reported jaunts to Randwick Racecourse are anything to go by.'

He smiled, appearing undaunted by her jibe. 'Odds of a million to one, I'd say, but then we were always drawn together. By the way, nice to know you've kept such a close eye on me via the newspapers. Miss me?'

She didn't have a chance to answer. To her amazement, he sat down, folding his long legs under the poky table. In doing so, their knees brushed, sending shock waves shooting up her legs.

'Why don't we have that drink I mentioned this afternoon?' He leaned towards her, creating an intimacy that drew her like a magnet.

'As I recall, I said no to your offer.'

His hypnotic stare bored right through to her soul.

'I know you didn't mean it. Anyway, let's just call this fate. We were destined to meet again and, now that we're both here, what's the harm in two old friends sharing a drink?'

Kara was lost in the liquid blue pools of his eyes, helpless to resist. She'd always been like this around him. Floundering. Lost. Yearning.

'Um, I'm actually meeting some people here shortly. Why don't we have that drink some other time?'

She had to fob him off before he discovered the real reason she was here and agreeing to a drink with him was a small price to pay.

'Actually, I'm one of those people you're waiting for.' He grinned, his confident smile revealing a row of even teeth that gleamed unnaturally white in the fluorescent lighting of the bar.

His answer floored her as realisation dawned. Matt, entering the agency this afternoon, Sal saying she had one more male applicant to screen, the co-incidental meeting at the bar tonight. No way! He'd been at Sal's on other business, surely?

'You're kidding? The great Matt Byrne, all-round party guy, can't get a date? Tell me the real reason you're here. Did Sal put you up to this?' She tried to keep the sarcasm out of her voice and failed.

He crossed his arms and leaned back, looking every inch the cool lawyer under interrogation.

'Don't be ridiculous. I found Sal's agency by chance. As for my being here tonight, I signed up this afternoon. I don't owe you any explanations, Kara. My life isn't an open book, so don't jump to conclusions.'

She persisted. 'But a dating agency? Why would a guy like you need help in getting a date?'

The words were out before she could think. Damn, now she would have to justify what she meant.

'A guy like me?' His voice dropped low, as tingles of excitement skittered down her spine.

'You know. Successful. Rich.' She glanced away, unable to match his stare.

'You forgot good-looking,' he teased.

Her cheeks warmed as she was forced to admit to the understatement of the year. 'Yeah, that too. So, what's your story?' She kept her tone flippant, hoping he was fooled. By the smug expression on his face, he wasn't.

'Not so fast. How about we enjoy our seven minutes together and if you want to know more, you'll have to choose me as your prospective date?'

She laughed. 'You're some piece of work! Blackmail will get you nowhere.'

He leaned forward. 'How about flattery? Will that get me anywhere?'

Suddenly eager to match wits with this intoxicating man, she batted her mascaraed eyelashes. 'You'll just have to try it and find out.'

His lips curved in a slow, seductive smile that melted any lingering resistance. 'You've got a deal.'

She leaned back and crossed her legs, giving Matt a tantalising glimpse of sheer stockings. He yearned to stroke every inch of her smooth flesh, caressing till she begged for more. Ever since he'd walked into the room, he could barely keep his eyes off her. Now he just had to convince his hands to do the same.

'So, do you know how tonight works?'

Even her rich voice seemed laden with sexy promise. He would have a hard time concentrating on anything she said over the next seven minutes if his thoughts persisted down this track. With an effort, he wrenched them back to the present.

'Yeah, Sally explained the routine to me. I spend seven minutes with seven gorgeous women, then choose my perfect match at the end. No laborious blind dates, no wasted small talk, no mindless chatter over dinners that seem to last an eternity. Just the way I wanted it.'

Kara glared at him. 'There's something you're not telling me. From all reports, you love dating. The more the merrier seems to be your motto. So why resort to this? I thought you were the type of guy who loves the thrill of the chase.'

'Sure, I love the chase as much as the next guy, but my priorities are changing.'

He hoped the answer would satisfy her. He wasn't ready to tell her the truth. He could barely face it himself.

She held her hands up in apparent surrender. He watched the long, elegant tapering of her fingers, imagining them stroking his body. Sitting here trying to look cool was becoming more difficult by the minute.

'Fine, whatever you say, Matt, though I still think you're up to something.' She laughed, a sweet, tinkling sound that revived memories of hot summer afternoons when they'd shared confidences and dreams. 'I'm looking forward to dragging your secrets from you, whether you like it or not.'

He reached across the table and captured her hand in his, sliding his thumb around her palm. 'I'm much more open to cajoling. Care to try?'

Kara swallowed, desperate to ease the sudden dryness in her throat. Matt's thumb created havoc with her senses, its swirling, concentric circles sending waves of pleasure through her body. She savoured his caress, all logic driven from her mind.

As she stared into his eyes, her stomach somersaulted. She wanted him. More than she had ever wanted anything in her life. Thank goodness tonight was a one-off. Matt Byrne was dangerous. In one day, he'd managed to revive feelings that she'd buried for years. He was far too much man for her to handle. Unfortunately, the thought of handling him conjured up more vivid images, flashing across her mind in an erotic kaleidoscope.

She pulled her hand away, needing to re-establish boundaries between them.

'I'm not here to cajole anything out of you. You'll tell me what's bugging you eventually. If not, I don't give a damn. Our friendship ended a long time ago, so why don't we get on with tonight's business and go our separate ways?'

He leaned back, crossed his arms and fixed her with a glare, leaving her feeling like a bug under a microscope. 'What makes you think that tonight will be the end of it?'

He smiled. Damn, she'd always had a hard time resisting that grin. She schooled her face into what she hoped was a mask of indifference. 'I'm not the one who quit our friendship, Matt. As I recall, it was all your decision when you pushed me away.'

The memory of his rejection still rankled. Pain like that lasted a lifetime. He'd been her first love. Her only love, if she was completely honest. And here he was after all this time, pretending that nothing had happened. She wouldn't make it easy for him.

'Can't we let bygones be bygones and move forward? Besides, you were just a kid back then. What did you expect me to do?'

To her annoyance, tears welled in her eyes. Tears of anger, shame and unmistakable regret.

'A kid? I was eighteen. Old enough to know what I wanted. Not that you cared. Apparently I was a pain in the ass, a little girl clinging to you, playing at being a vamp, with a hell of a lot of growing up to do. Do those words ring any bells?' She blinked furiously, wishing the tears away.

He ran his hand through his hair, a tell-tale sign he was rattled.

'I'm sorry, Kara. I'd just finished law school and was doing my articles. I had a lot on my mind and didn't need the attentions of a schoolgirl, hell-bent on experimentation…' He trailed off as she leaped to her feet.

'Who the hell do you think you are? I wasn't experimenting, I was in—'

'Hey, you two. We're about to start. What's with the fireworks?' Sally materialised at their table, hands on hips, a frown marring her forehead.

'Sal, I need to talk to you.' Kara grabbed her arm and dragged Sally away from the table.

'I can't do this,' she hissed. 'Matt is driving me insane. You can't expect me to spend another second with him, let alone the next seven minutes.'

Sally smiled, her calmness doing little to soothe Kara's frazzled nerves. 'Calm down, dear. I know tonight is an ordeal for you. Just do it for me. Please?'

Kara took a deep breath and exhaled. There was no way she could resist the beseeching look in Sal's eyes.

'OK. I'll do this for you. But I swear, as soon as I've spoken to the last moronic man, I'm out of here!'

'That's my girl. Now, take a seat, smile at Matt, make small talk and the torture will be over before you know it.'

Kara turned to face Matt. He hadn't moved an inch, and by the amused look on his face he'd heard every word of their conversation.

'All sorted out?' he enquired softly.

'Mmm,' she mumbled. 'We're about to get started. Good luck, Matt. I hope you find what, or should I say who, you're looking for tonight.'

'What if I've already found her?'

'I'd say good luck to her. She's going to need it. Thank goodness we've established I'm not your type.'

A hint of uncertainty flickered in his eyes. 'Lucky, huh? Who knows what would've happened if I hadn't pushed you away all those years ago?'

Kara had a fair idea and she didn't feel lucky at all.

About an hour later, the ordeal was over. She could hardly remember speaking to the various men as only one man's words echoed in her mind. Matt had held her enthralled for their seven minutes together, flirting with the practice of a man seasoned to the art.

Sure, she'd resisted. However, it had been like holding back a flood with a few sandbags. No chance. Despite their earlier confrontation, all accusations had been put aside as he'd focused his attention solely and squarely on her.

No woman could resist Matt Byrne at his best: flashing smile, mesmerising eyes, animated conversation. He'd drawn her in like a spider coaxed a fly into its web. Trapping her, whether she liked it or not. Seven minutes had passed in an instant. That was his power. He could make time seem insignificant, his voice wrapping its seductive tones around her, holding her spellbound.

The rest of the men had paled in comparison. She couldn't recall one word of the other conversations, though each man had been polite and a good conversationalist. Kara knew that her poor recollection had everything to do with her wandering attention as she'd watched Matt ensnare the other women with his charm.

A tight coil of tension had wound deep in her belly as she watched each and every woman fall under his spell. Who could blame them? She'd done the same thing, despite her vow of playing it cool. Who would be the lucky lady? she wondered. Her bets were on the busty brunette who had hung on his every word, patting him on the arm at regular intervals.

Kara had wanted to tear her eyes out. The brunette was just his type, all silicone and pouty lips. She'd seen enough similar women draped over him in the newspapers, annoyed at her irrational jealousy over each and every one. Men were so predictable.

Kara stared at the form lying on the table. Even though it was a formality, her hand shook as she ticked the 'yes' box next to Matt's name. After their earlier verbal sparring, there was no way he would choose her so she was safe in marking his name. It would be just her luck to mark some other random guy and end up matched with him. No way, no how. Sal's computer could work its magic on some other sucker. There was only so far she would go to help Sal out.

The brunette would select Matt and vice versa. The sooner the thousandth couple matched was announced, the sooner she could escape. Matt and the brunette. Her gut clenched at the thought.

Sally whisked her form away, adding it to the pile in her hand. She winked. 'Not long now, possum, and you can head home. Thanks a million. Love you.'

'Love you too,' Kara murmured, scanning the room for signs of Matt. He was deep in conversation with the brunette. Still. Hadn't anyone told them that their seven minutes were up?

She turned away, wishing the evening would end. In a way, seeing Matt had been a nice surprise. Seeing him all over other women was not so nice.

Seeing him matched with a dark version of Pamela Anderson would be too much.

'Can I have your attention, ladies and gentlemen? Matchmaker has successfully matched nine hundred and ninety-nine couples over the last few years. Speed dating is the exciting, quick, non-pressured way to meet singles with similar interests, so if you haven't met your match tonight, please come back again.'

Sally paused, nodding and smiling at the applauding crowd. 'Now, without further ado, Matchmaker is proud to announce its thousandth couple matched.'

A strange churning started deep in Kara's gut. She couldn't watch the elation on the lucky woman's face, for she had no doubt that Matt would be the man chosen tonight.

'Would Matt Byrne and Kara Roberts please come up here?'

Kara sat riveted to her seat, stunned. She could have sworn that Sal had just announced her name. There had to be a mistake. The churning increased tenfold as she watched Matt stalk towards her.

'Kara, I think they want us.'

She stared at his outstretched hand as if it were a cobra. If she placed her hand in his, she'd be lost. Her lips moved, the stiffness in her facial muscles easing into the semblance of a smile. She could do this. She had to.

'That's my girl,' he whispered as he squeezed her hand and guided her towards the stage.

She moved mechanically, placing one foot in front of the other, oblivious to the hoots and congratulations coming from all directions.

Sally patted her arm as she reached the stage and whispered in her ear. 'Sorry, love. You and Matt were the only two that matched. I couldn't fudge the results. The agency board checks into details like that, not to mention the fact that several of the award judges are here. Forgive me?'

With the blood pounding in her head, Kara stared at Sally. Strangely, she didn't look at all remorseful. In fact, she looked downright happy! However, there was little time to argue the point now. There were more important things to worry about, like how she could end this farce without jeopardising Sal's business in the process. And how she could deflect Matt's attentions when he'd just chosen her as his most desirable partner.

As if reading her mind, Matt murmured, 'Just go with the flow for now.'

Kara stared, the intensity of his gaze doing little to calm her.

Easier said than done.

CHAPTER THREE

THE bar cleared once the formalities were over. Kara smiled and accepted the congratulations of the other participants with Matt hanging on to her hand the entire time. By the time the last person had left, her face ached with the effort of maintaining a look of happiness. Happiness? Nothing could be further from the truth. It was time to sort this mess out, once and for all.

'Matt, could we talk? By the way, you can let go of my hand now. The charade's over.'

She watched the warmth in his eyes fade as he dropped her hand. 'Would you like a drink? By the look on your face, I think I'm going to need one.'

She didn't like the hardened edge in his voice, though she could cope with it more easily than his friendliness. This was going to be difficult enough.

'A small white wine, please. I'll meet you at the corner table.'

'Choosing the most secluded table in the place? Either you're going to tell me how thrilled you are to be my chosen date or you're planning to ditch me. Which one is it?'

She stiffened, once again startled at his apparent ability to read her mind.

'Yeah, I thought as much. Going to make me pay for what happened nine years ago, aren't you?' He turned towards the waiting barman. 'A white wine and an orange juice for me, please. On second thoughts, make mine a scotch.'

Rather than heading to the table, Kara waited. She watched Matt run his hand through his hair, glance at his wrist-watch and tap his foot against the polished floor. It looked as if he couldn't wait to get out of here and she knew the feeling. Why on earth had he chosen her?

Sure, she was flattered. What woman wouldn't be? Matt's imposing persona drew women in droves and she was no exception. Even now, when he looked impatient, there was no hiding his potent aura behind an expensive navy suit and an ivory silk shirt. The stylish clothes did little to detract from his broad chest, tapering to a lean waist and long legs. She guessed the shirt hid a washboard stomach too. No doubt Matt would look just as impressive without his clothes.

Her imagination took full flight as she fantasised what he would look like without them.

'Planning your line of attack?'

His interruption brought her back to the present

but didn't calm her galloping pulse. She had to get her body under control if she was to do this.

'I'm not a client, Matt. No line of attack. I just want to talk,' she snapped, striding towards the table, more annoyed at her body's irrational response than at him.

Matt watched her flounce ahead, head held high. Whatever happened to the quiet, shy Kara he'd known? He'd thought she would be happy that he chose her. Not out of ego but from some warped sense that she'd been just as eager as he to restart their friendship. Apparently not. So much for his sure-fire lawyer's instinct to read people. This time his judgement had been way off and the thought rattled him.

'Here you are. White wine, as ordered.'

He stared at her butt as she slid into her seat. Man, she was a stunner. The black dress she wore clung to every curve of her body, hugging in all the right places. Her large breasts gave the impression of a tiny waist, leading to those endless, long legs. Once again, his mind raced with sexy images. He had it bad.

Remember, this is a business arrangement.

'Tell that to my libido,' he muttered as he took a sip of whisky.

'Pardon?'

Now she was staring at him with those luminous

green eyes. Convincing his libido was going to be harder than he thought.

'Nothing. Now, what did you want to discuss?'

Kara took a steadying breath. With Matt staring at her as if she was his next meal, it was difficult to concentrate on the task at hand.

'We need to sort out this situation. I'm not interested in dating anybody at the moment. The only reason I was here tonight was to help Sal make up the numbers.' She smoothed the folds of her skirt to stop her hands fidgeting. 'Anyway, perhaps we can chat to Sal and you can pair up with one of the other ladies?'

'No.'

She squirmed under the scrutiny of his disconcerting stare.

'I chose you for a reason, Kara. You're just the kind of woman I'm after.'

'And what kind of woman is that?'

He placed his fingertips together, leaned his elbows on the table and stared directly into her eyes. 'Smart, independent, with no illusions. From our conversation earlier, you have no romantic interest in me whatsoever. In fact, you even knocked back the opportunity to catch up for a drink this afternoon. So, you're the perfect choice for me.'

Confusion whirled through her mind. 'I don't get it.'

He smiled, though it didn't reach his eyes. In fact, they had darkened to a cold, icy blue. 'Your apparent dislike of me is exactly what I'm looking for. There will be no misconceptions on your part, no chance of you falling for me and wrecking the deal. For that's all this dating business will be. A deal. A business arrangement. Nothing more. You will appear as my steady girlfriend for the next six months, till I secure a partnership in Dad's firm. That's it.'

His cold stare reinforced the bleakness in his voice. He had the tone down pat. She knew exactly how his opposition would feel in the courtroom. Coerced. Beaten. Devastated. And she'd been foolish enough to think he might still harbour unresolved feelings for her. What a joke!

'So what do I get out of this so-called deal? Do you think I can be bought?' She steadied her voice, reluctant to give him any advantage.

'Everyone can be bought. It's just the price that varies.'

Kara cringed. 'When did you become so cynical?'

'Not cynical, merely realistic. I see the purchasing power of money every day, not to mention first-hand with my dad.' He spat the words out as if they were poison.

'Your dad?'

'He's the perfect example of what money can buy. Just ask his latest wife. Wife number three, twenty years younger than him and as money-grabbing as they come. Sad, isn't it?' His lip curled, as if he'd just seen something repulsive. 'Anyway, enough about my family. What's it to be?'

Thoughts raced through her mind. If she accepted Matt's bizarre offer in exchange for money, her problems would be solved. She could save Matchmaker by securing the DATY award for Sally and then concentrate on boosting her own business. For money was the only thing she could think of to keep this deal concrete, unemotional and one hundred per cent business.

'Fine. I accept, Matt. I'll appear as your girlfriend for six months, for thirty thousand dollars.'

He flinched, then quickly recovered. 'Deal. I'll draw up a contract in the morning. Can you come past my office around ten?'

Kara nodded. 'I've got an appointment at Bondi around eleven. Will it take long?'

'My office is in town, so no, it should be quick and painless.'

She wondered if he meant the contract signing, the trip or the deal. He downed his drink in three short gulps and stood up.

'Do you need a lift home?'

She shook her head. 'No, thanks, I have my car here.'

He opened his wallet and handed her a business

card. 'In that case, here are my details. I'll see you tomorrow.'

As she reached for the card, their fingers brushed. Matt pulled back as if scalded, an unreadable expression in his eyes.

'See you then.'

She watched him stride towards the door without looking back. Sipping at her wine, Kara relished the icy liquid sliding down her parched throat. The evening hadn't gone to plan and there wasn't one damn thing she could have done about it. Apart from say no to his deal. And leave Sal in the lurch? No way. She would pay her dues.

Then why did she feel as if she'd just made a deal with the devil himself?

CHAPTER FOUR

KARA entered the impressive offices of Byrne and Associates. She glanced around the reception area, enclosed by floor-to-ceiling glass overlooking Sydney. It screamed wealth: polished floorboards, cream leather chairs, Pro Hart paintings strategically placed on the walls. No expense spared.

The receptionist fitted the image too: sleek, well-groomed and sharp as a pin. 'May I help you?'

'Yes, Matt Byrne is expecting me. I'm Kara Roberts.'

'I'll inform Mr Byrne you've arrived.' She smiled at Kara as she punched buttons on the phone console. 'Ms Roberts to see you, Mr Byrne.'

She stood up and beckoned Kara. 'Please follow me.'

Kara admired the expensive cut of the receptionist's designer suit, glad about her own choice of outfit. Today had definitely called for power dressing so she'd chosen a chic red suit teamed with a black polo neck and black accessories. Sally said the look intimidated people, especially men. Therefore, she reserved it for clinching deals with particularly difficult

male clients. She figured Matt now fell into that category.

She thanked the receptionist as she knocked on the
door bearing the shiny plaque MATTHEW BYRNE.

'Come in.'

Kara pasted a bright smile on her face as she
opened the door, ignoring the rampaging butterflies
in her stomach.

'Good morning, Matt. How are you?'

He looked up from a mountain of paperwork and
glanced at his watch. 'Right on ten. I like a woman
who's punctual.'

As he stood and walked towards her the butterflies
in her stomach took flight. He looked incredible. The
charcoal pinstriped suit, deep blue shirt and matching
tie combined to lend him the look of a professional
man exuding power. The shirt matched the stunning
blue of his eyes, which were fixed on her at that
moment.

'Would you like a coffee?'

'No, thanks. I haven't got time. I have an appointment at eleven, remember?' She didn't want to be
churlish but that was exactly how her reply sounded.
Mean and ungrateful.

'Fine. Let's get down to business. Here's the contract. Take a look; let me know what you think.'

Kara took the paper he handed her and sat down,
carefully smoothing her skirt so it wouldn't ride up

her thighs. Her sixth sense was on full alert. Matt
didn't return to his chair. Instead he leaned against
the desk, watching her. Every inch of her body could
sense his gaze yet she refused to look at him.
Besides, she needed to concentrate to decipher the
contract.

Legalities frightened her, the clauses and provisos
endless. However, this document seemed straightfor-
ward. Matt hadn't used too much jargon and she understood the gist of it. He was buying her as his
girlfriend for thirty thousand dollars. A small price
to pay for Sal's peace of mind. And her own.

Not that she had any intention of taking the money
for herself. She would figure something out to save
her business. This was just to payback Sal.

'Where do I sign?' She risked a glance at Matt.
Warring expressions she couldn't quite fathom flitted
across his face.

He removed a pen from his top pocket. He leaned
over and pointed to the contract. 'Right on the dotted
line.'

Kara stared blankly at the document. Her brain
wouldn't function with Matt leaning over her, his
tangy aftershave enveloping her in a sensuous cloud.
Heat radiated off his body, or was it the languorous
warmth seeping through her own that made her want
to rip her clothes off as the temperature around them
reached boiling point?

'Kara?'

Even the way he uttered her name sounded like a silken caress. Desire flowed through her body, screaming for release. No man had ever made her feel this way. What the heck was going on? She didn't like feeling this out of control.

Her hand shook as she signed the contract.

'There. All done.' She stood quickly, eager to escape the confines of his office. Unfortunately, her legs were as shaky as the rest of her and she swayed, reaching for the desk.

'I've got you,' Matt murmured as he grabbed her upper arms. 'Are you OK?'

She preferred his icy disdain of last night. The concern radiating from his eyes right now would undo her in a second.

Unable to speak or tear her gaze away, she nodded.

'Don't you think we can find a better way to seal our deal? After all, you're my new girlfriend.' His smile was slow, warm, seductive.

Kara's heart skipped a beat. She couldn't bear his proximity any longer yet somehow she couldn't find the will to move. *Warning, danger,* flashed through her mind. If she didn't establish the boundaries of their relationship right here, right now, there would be trouble with a capital T.

'I'm only your girlfriend in public. We're not on show at the moment.'

Where had that voice come from? All soft and breathy? An answering flicker of heat glowed in his eyes. 'I know, honey, but there's no harm in practising. After all, practice makes perfect.'

He stared at her lips, lowering his head as if in slow motion. She closed her eyes and tilted her head, powerless to stop the wheels in motion. All logic deserted her when his lips brushed hers in a feather-light kiss.

'I thought the saying was prolonged practice makes perfect,' she whispered against the side of his mouth.

In that instant, she was lost. His lips crushed hers in a mind-blowing, earth-shattering assault on her senses. His tongue coaxed and flicked as he nibbled and sucked at her bottom lip. She opened her mouth, allowing him full access, revelling in the sinuous, erotic dance of their tongues. Her hands snaked around his neck as he pulled her flush against the hard length of his body.

This was the type of kiss she'd dreamed about, the kiss that she'd craved on her eighteenth birthday and for years since. Her body took on a life of its own as she moulded to him, savouring every glorious inch of contact.

As she leaned into him, Matt groaned and

wrenched his mouth away. Kara stared at him and stepped back, tugging at her jacket. What on earth had possessed her to provoke him like that? She'd practically invited that kiss. And she'd wanted to appear cool, in control. Hah! What a joke! Her traitorous body had put paid to that idea. How could she last six months pretending to be his girlfriend when she couldn't push him away on the first day?

The kiss had dissolved any ideas she'd harboured about her self-control and disdain of his deal. She'd talked herself into believing that Matt was pathetic, having to buy the company of a woman to secure a partnership in his dad's firm. She'd also scoffed at ideas that she still loved him, attributing her reawakened feelings to a teenage crush. *Sure.* She was the pathetic one.

'I must go, Matt.'

Her heart flip-flopped at the bewildered look on his face.

He strode around the desk, obviously keen to put as much space between them as possible. 'I'll be in touch. I've got several dinner engagements over the next few weeks and we'll need to co-ordinate schedules.'

'Fine, give me a call.' She paused. 'Matt, about that kiss—'

'Don't worry about it. Look at it as a novel way to seal a deal.' He barely glanced her way as he thrust the contract she'd just signed into a manila folder. 'I'll call you.'

Feeling suitably chastised and dismissed, Kara walked out of the room. Only once she'd closed the door and leaned against it did she realise she'd been holding her breath. She exhaled in relief, though it was short-lived.

If that kiss had sealed the contract, she suddenly wished that she'd read the fine print a lot more carefully…

CHAPTER FIVE

KARA slammed her front door shut and kicked off her heels. Her briefcase dropped with a resounding thud and she sank into the comfy cushions of the sofa, leaned back and closed her eyes.

What a day. Ever since she'd signed Matt's stupid contract this morning, things had spiralled downhill. Fast.

She'd been caught up in roadworks on the way to Bondi, which delayed her appointment by half an hour. Penelope, the snobbish wife of media mogul Jack Normanby, had berated her for the next hour despite the fact she'd apologised for not calling. She still couldn't believe she'd let herself get so wound up about her meeting with Matt this morning that she had forgotten to charge her mobile phone.

To make matters worse, Penelope and her delinquent teenage daughter had scoffed at every idea she'd put forward for the redecoration of their palatial home. When Penelope's mother-in-law arrived and joined in the act, she'd drawn on every reserve of tact she possessed. But the three of them had been like a tag team.

'Darling Penelope, don't you think chintz is sooo gauche?'

'Oh, no, Mother, it's positively divine. Don't you think Kara's ideas are quaint? After all, she is the expert.'

At this, Mother dearest had looked down her nose at Kara, as if she were something the family corgi had just dragged in.

'Well, only if you're sure, Penelope. Daddy and I have other contacts if this one doesn't suit.'

She'd smiled politely, thinking of the whopping commission…and then proceeded to pull childish faces the moment they'd turned their Gucci-clad backs.

After leaving the three women to their own devices, she'd returned to the office, only to find gremlins in her computer and a pile of unfinished quotes. Even Olivia, her trusty PA, had turned on her in her hour of need. Olivia had picked up the latest issue of the *Financial Times*, the one with Kara's ex, Steve Rockwell, the up-and-coming lawyer, plastered across the front, and proceeded to sing his praises.

Unfortunately, while she was thinking about lawyers, Matt's virile image flashed into her mind. Once it was there, she couldn't dislodge it and Olivia had picked up on it.

'What's up? You've got *that* look. The one you

get every time you see a picture of Mel Gibson in a magazine. All glassy-eyed and gooey.'

'I don't know what you're talking about. Besides, I haven't drooled over Mel for at least a month.'

Sure, she'd refuted Olivia's claims. However, once Matt had insinuated his way into her thoughts, there was no escaping. She'd replayed their kiss a thousand times, reliving every touch, taste and nuance. Finally, after cursing the computer and staring blankly at the quotes for an hour, she'd called it a day.

Not that being home relieved her tension. If anything, her whirlwind thoughts were sucking her in deeper. Massaging her temples, she inhaled and exhaled deep breaths, willing her mind and body to relax. It was just a kiss…just a kiss… If she repeated the mantra often enough, she might start to believe it.

The telephone's harsh ring shattered her momentary peace.

'Hello, Kara speaking,' she all but snapped into the receiver.

'Just the woman I'm after.' Matt's husky tone did little to soothe her frayed nerves. 'How was your day? And why the attitude?'

'My day was a disaster, if you must know. From start to finish.' She sounded childish yet didn't care.

He was the last person she wanted to speak to right now.

'That bad, huh? Even your morning?'

To her horror, something akin to a snort exploded from her nose. 'Particularly the morning. It set the tone for the whole day. Thanks to our meeting I was late to a very important appointment.'

'I'm sorry to hear that, though our meeting didn't run all that long. As I recall, our business was short and sweet.' His rich voice ran over her like a caress. 'You haven't forgotten our deal, have you?'

The deal had been a cinch but heat flooded her at the memory of the method in which they had sealed it.

'Of course not. Is that why you're calling? Time to get some value for money?'

She regretted the words as soon as they left her mouth. The silence on the other end of the line was ominous. Now, rather than feeling hot and bothered, she felt her stomach quiver.

'How perceptive of you, sweetheart.' His voice was cold and sent a chill down her spine. 'I've got a business dinner tonight so I'll pick you up at eight. If this morning was any indication, I'd say you'll be giving me more than my money's worth. I can't wait to see what you do when the deal is near completion.'

'You bast—'

'Uh-uh. I'll see you at eight. And wear something dressy.'

The steady hum of the dial tone rang in her ears. She stared at the phone, speechless. Muttering a string of unladylike curses, she slammed the receiver back on the hook and stomped into the bedroom. How dared he speak to her like that? She already felt like a commodity, a possession to be told when they would be going out and where. She just didn't like hearing it from him.

She stripped and flung her clothes on the bed. Shaking, she wrenched the gold hoops from her ears, snagging her top in the process.

'Blast!' She muttered, fiddling with the delicate clasp on the earring. It gave way, snapping in two.

She sank onto the bed, dropped her head in her hands and cried, loud, rolling sobs that echoed in the silence. Sure, tears were childish and made her feel more than a tad stupid, but they were cathartic. The earring was replaceable but her sanity wasn't. Ever since she'd signed on the dotted line, she'd been acting crazy. The kiss had just been the start.

She'd been a monster on the phone just now, taking out her frustrations on Matt. Not that he hadn't deserved some of it. After all, she wouldn't be a basket case right now if it weren't for him.

Six months. Right now, it seemed like a life sentence. How could she pretend to be his girlfriend when all she'd ever dreamed of was to be the real thing? Their relationship was strained at best. Would people see through the charade? What then? Would Matt dump her in search of the next woman he could buy? For that was all she was, really. An acquisition he'd purchased. God, he must think she was cheap.

What do you care what he thinks? Think of Sal. You owe her.

The thought of Sally did it. She dried her tears and strode into the bathroom, eager to wash away her woes. She could do this. If Matt thought of her as a purchase, that was exactly what she would give him. An attractive package, something he could show off to his shallow business colleagues. And if he expected anything else from her, he could whistle for it.

Matt rang the bell and waited. He glanced around, noting the attractive blend of cream and heritage red paint adorning the two-storey terrace house. Neat rows of box hedges surrounded a small patch of lawn, the lush green broken by strategically planted petunias. The entrance path was flanked by large terracotta pots which blended perfectly with the overall colour scheme. His eye for detail annoyed him at times; it helped in his line of work, but he couldn't turn it off. Kara was talented, he'd give her that much. If the outside looked this good, the inside would be amazing.

He admired her success. She'd always wanted to be a designer, ever since she'd rearranged Sally's house at the age of fourteen. She'd transformed the drab interior into a work of art with seemingly little effort. He hadn't been so impressed when she'd turned her attentions to co-ordinating his wardrobe.

He wrenched his thoughts back to the present as the door opened.

'Hi, Matt. Right on time.' Her sexy voice sent his imagination into overdrive. Where the hell had that come from? She hadn't sounded like that on the phone earlier. Far from it.

He struggled not to gape. She was a vision, wrapped in a green material that hugged every curve of her exquisite body and fell in soft folds to her knees. He had a difficult time tearing his gaze away from a tantalising glimpse of cleavage, which hinted at the lushness beneath. She'd piled her hair high on her head, a few loose curls framing her face. He disliked make-up, yet she'd used just a smidgeon to highlight her wide eyes and full mouth. The results were stunning.

'You look gorgeous,' he murmured, noting the slight blush that stained her cheeks. That was one habit she definitely hadn't grown out of and he loved it.

'Thanks. Ready to go?'

He nodded, not trusting himself to speak as she turned to close the door. Her legs were encased in the sheerest stockings, a light sheen drawing further attention to their length.

'So, where are we going tonight?'

She stared at him, waiting for an answer. The problem was, he couldn't remember the question. He'd been too busy indulging in the delightful fantasy of peeling those stockings from her long legs and kissing his way from her ankles upwards.

'Sorry, what did you say?' *Good one, Byrne. Real smooth.*

Thankfully, she laughed, the same laugh that had taunted him all those years ago and his response was almost visceral. 'Earth to Matt. Are you OK?'

'Yeah, just distracted.' And that was only the half of it. 'The dinner tonight is important. One of the firm's competitors is honing in on our staff and I need to put a stop to it.'

He didn't add the part about his father perhaps taking him more seriously if he could achieve this.

'Isn't that unethical?' She raised an eyebrow.

He shrugged. 'Yeah, though nothing surprises me any more in the corporate world. It's like being surrounded by a school of piranhas. One false step and you're a goner.'

'Sounds like some of my clientele,' she chuckled. 'I can empathise one hundred per cent.'

Matt joined in her laughter as he opened the car door for her. This was more like it. He'd missed their rapport, the easygoing camaraderie. If they could sustain this level of friendship for the next six months, the task ahead was going to be a piece of cake.

'Nice car. It's very *you*.'

Kara glanced around the modern interior, inhaling the rich scent of new leather.

'What does that mean?'

The engine idled quietly as he stared at her. She couldn't think when he looked at her like that: intense, probing, with just a hint of scepticism.

'Don't be so defensive. I just meant that a silver sports car screams status and that's what you've wanted your whole life. That's why I'm here isn't it, so you can convince Jeff you're partner material?' She could've bitten her tongue. Whenever she spoke to him, her words sounded judgemental. So much for her plan to appear cool.

For a moment, his eyes glittered and his jaw clenched.

'Yes, that's why you're here, so let's go.'

An uncomfortable silence yawned between them. Kara sneaked several peeks at his profile while pretending to look at the passing scenery. Lord, he was something. Not just handsome but drop-dead gorgeous, the type of guy who made women believe in male harems. Yet another designer suit encased his impressive body, black this time, with a crisp white shirt underneath. The guy had style…and then some. Breathing was a difficult task in the confines of his car as an intoxicating waft of woody aftershave hit her reeling senses. Walking away from him in six months was going to be hell.

'See anything you like?'

His question startled her. So much for subtlety. He'd been fully aware of her wandering eyes the entire time. Tired of the tension, she came to a quick decision. For the rest of the night, she would make an effort to keep the conversation light. No barbs. No judgements.

'Maybe, though I think a closer look is in order.'

His low laughter rumbled like thunder. She loved storms: fierce, impressive, spectacular. Just like Matt.

'I think that can be arranged. How close do you need to get?' His lowered voice rasped across her nerve endings, firing her imagination with thoughts of getting up close and personal with the man of her dreams.

'Real close,' she murmured, her pulse quickening in anticipation.

'Do you mean that or are you just getting into character?'

'Pardon?'

'Take a look around. We're here. I just thought you were practising the girlfriend role.'

She glanced around in surprise. She'd been so wrapped up in the intimate cocoon of the car and their flirtation that she'd failed to notice the car had stopped.

'Yeah, that was it.' She hoped that the tell-tale blush wouldn't betray her as her body burned at his teasing words. God, if he only knew where her thoughts had been before he stopped the car.

He merely stared at her for a moment longer than necessary before turning away. 'I thought so. You played the seductive girlfriend role so well, you'll have to add ''actress'' to your list of talents. For a moment you had me fooled.'

Tell him it's true. Tell him you do want to get up close and personal. Now's your chance.

Instead, she opened the door and stepped out. 'Oh, I'm a woman of many talents. The sooner you work that out, the better.'

'Women,' he muttered, locking the car with a particularly vicious stab at the remote. When he looked up, his cool stare doused her fiery imagination like a bucket of cold water.

So much for getting along.

'Tonight's important to me. Thanks for being here.'

She noted the uncertainty flicker across his striking face, lending it a vulnerability that touched her heart.

'No problem,' she replied flippantly. If she kept her cool, there would be little chance of dropping her defences again. Let him flirt all he liked, she'd be ready for him.

However, as she tried to ignore her racing pulse at the touch of his guiding hand in the small of her back, Kara realised there was a problem. A huge problem. And he was walking straight towards them.

CHAPTER SIX

'SO, HOW'S my favourite interior designer these days?'

Steve Rockwell kissed her cheek and Kara's first instinct was to pull away. Instead, she schooled her features into a polite mask and smiled.

'Fine, thanks, Steve. How are you?'

'All the better for seeing you. You're looking stunning as usual.'

His compliment made her uncomfortable, considering Matt was standing right next to her. She squirmed under Steve's scrutiny. He'd always made her feel this way, awkward and not good enough. Her only comfort was the feel of Matt's firm hand in the small of her back. She ignored the compliment. He hadn't changed a bit. The same unruly blond hair, grey eyes, immaculate suit and smooth words. He looked a millions bucks and he knew it. Pity he didn't have a heart.

There was an awkward pause before she rushed on, 'I'd like you to meet a friend of mine. Steve, this is Matt Byrne.'

Steve glared at Matt, his eyes turning an icy pewter. 'What are you doing here, Byrne? Crawl out from under your rock again?'

Her stomach twisted in surprise. Her head swivelled between both men and she saw Matt's usual mask of composure slip as he tightened his grip on her back.

'Nice to see you, too, Rockwell. Haven't lost any of your charm, I see.' The coldness in his voice could have frozen the Antarctic twice over.

'Why would I waste my charm on the likes of you? I'd rather focus it on the lovely woman at your side.'

Matt slid an arm around her shoulders and hugged her closer. Kara had no option other than to snuggle. 'That's the smartest thing you've said in a long while, Rockwell. Kara isn't just lovely, she's warm, gorgeous and funny. She's also my girlfriend.'

Steve snorted. 'Poor girl. Obviously doesn't know you too well. How long till you chalk her up as conquest number one hundred?'

Matt's fingers dug into Kara's shoulder. 'Careful, Rockwell—'

'Whoa! I'm still here, guys. As much as I'd like to stay and chat, I'm leaving you to sort out which boy has the biggest toy. Matt, I'll see you inside.'

Kara strode away, head held high, hoping her knees would hold out till she reached the safety of the restaurant. Fury surged through her body. She wasn't a prize to be flaunted and she'd be damned if she ended up as a notch on anyone's bedpost.

'Hey, wait up!' Matt grabbed her arm and spun her around. 'What was all that about?'

Kara wrenched her arm free. 'I'm not your current "show and tell" exhibit, you know.'

His eyes narrowed. 'Have you forgotten our little agreement? Perhaps you need reminding?'

Before she could utter a word, his lips crushed hers in an all-demanding, consuming kiss. There was no tender giving, no seduction. It was a commanding kiss, his tongue insinuating its way into her mouth while his hands moulded to her behind and pulled her against him. Resistance was a fleeting thought and quickly discarded as she clung to him, allowing her own hands the freedom to slip beneath his jacket and caress the hard contours of his chest. His heat radiated through the crisp cotton, drawing her in like the ocean on a hot summer's day.

The kiss deepened as his tongue coaxed its way into her mouth. She was burning up, the darting tip taking her excitement up a notch. There was nothing else but his tongue, his hands, his body.

It took several seconds for the slow applause to penetrate her passion-hazed mind.

'Well done. Nice display, you two. Pity you weren't into exhibitionism when you were with me,

Kara. Would've made our love life a whole lot more fun.'

Matt clenched his fists and she sensed he was itching to punch her supercilious ex right on his patrician nose.

'Don't you ever speak to Kara like that again,' Matt said quietly, his barely controlled anger evident in the set of his jaw.

She didn't know whether to laugh or cry. The scene was ludicrous, like something out of a B-grade movie. 'Let's go, Matt.'

She tugged at his jacket. He glanced at her in surprise, as if he'd forgotten she was even there.

'Sure. Just one more thing.' He looked towards Steve, derision etched into every line of his powerful face. 'Stay the hell out of my way, Rockwell, and leave Kara alone.'

At that, Steve spun on his heel and walked away.

'Are you OK?' she murmured, reaching out and smoothing his curled fingers till he relaxed.

'Yeah. What about you?'

'Hey, I wasn't the one about to swing the punches.'

He had the grace to look sheepish. 'Sorry about that. I just saw red when he said that stuff about you. My fist almost took on a life of its own.' He sank to his haunches and dropped his head in his hands.

'Dammit, I'm becoming more like my father every day. Act first, think later.'

Kara thought she must have heard wrong. Jeff Byrne was a lovely man, hard but fair. Surely he wasn't into physical violence?

'What did you say?' she asked, almost afraid of the answer.

He stood up quickly and brushed his suit off. 'Nothing. How involved were you and Rockwell?'

She shrugged. 'We dated on and off for a while.'

'How long?' he persisted.

'Two years.' It sounded impossibly long even to her own ears.

'Two years? You're kidding! That's not dating, that's a marriage.'

'It was a few years ago. I was young.'

'So does that mean you're old and wise now?'

'Old, yes. Wise, no. I'm posing as your girlfriend for thirty thousand dollars, you keep kissing me and I've just condoned your caveman-like behaviour. Does that sound wise to you?'

She couldn't fathom the expression in his eyes. 'Only the kissing part.' He took hold of her hand. 'Let's forget this mess for tonight. I need you by my side, nothing more, nothing less. Are you happy with that?'

She shook her head, wondering what on earth had possessed her to sign that contract. 'No, I'm not happy. This whole situation is ludicrous. You, me, the contract, the money. However, a deal's a deal and if you need my help I'm here for you.'

'What about the money? Would you be willing to help me if the cash wasn't an issue?'

She hesitated. 'N-no, I probably wouldn't.' How could she tell him the money was a cold, hard fact she was using to keep this deal emotion-free?

The bleakness in his eyes cut to her core. It was gone in a second, replaced by a heart-wrenching hardness. It was so quick that she doubted if it had been there at all.

'Fine. At least we're both being honest here. Shall we go inside? Time to start earning your fee.'

She bit her top lip, fighting back tears. Tonight was only the beginning. He was right; he'd purchased her company and it was time to start paying up.

'I thought tonight was a success,' Kara said lightly.

'Depends on your definition of success.' Matt sounded angry but didn't care. Success was the furthest thing from his mind when she stared at him like that, all wide-eyed innocence. He wanted to finish what they'd started earlier. That kiss had been the prelude to a tantalising overture, and boy, did he want the rousing finale.

'Well, your colleagues seemed to accept me and

you gained the information you were after.' Her voice was soft, tentative. Combined with her bewitching eyes, it tugged at his heart till he couldn't think straight. All he could do was feel, which was exactly what he didn't want. Or need. This was business, pure and simple. *Think about the partnership. Stay focused. Keep your cool.*

'Would you like to come sailing with me tomorrow?'

Yeah, that should keep things cool. Just you and the hottest woman on the planet wearing bathing suits on a secluded yacht? Real cool.

His heart lurched as her face lit up. 'I'd love to. Remember that summer when your handmade masterpiece tipped me in the lake?'

He chuckled. 'Yeah, I remember. That canoe was an example of nautical brilliance.'

'You could've fooled me! It took my new white T-shirt hours to dry off.'

'Exactly.'

He saw her pupils dilate as a hint of pink stained her smooth cheeks. God, she was incredible.

'Come on, let's get out of here.' He held her hand as they farewelled his various business acquaintances, a strange pride filling him. She'd been outstanding tonight, almost convincing him at one point that she was a woman in love. If only she'd agreed to be his girlfriend without the money. She could have named any other price, just not the damn money. Gold-diggers just weren't his style.

'Can I ask you something?'

'Sure.' He opened the car door for her, studiously avoiding looking at her legs. He'd seen the way her dress had ridden up earlier in the evening when she'd slid into the car. Sheer heaven. Right now, he was less than impressed with his careening emotions and he knew that one more glimpse would make him do something stupid. He'd wanted a simple business arrangement. Where had the invitation to go sailing come from?

'Why do you want this partnership so badly?'

The engine purred to life as he turned the key. 'I need to prove a lot of things to a lot of people.' He didn't want to talk about this, not here, not now. He hoped his curt answer would stop her from asking any more.

'Does your father fall into that category?'

'Yes.'

He switched the CD player on. The soft crooning of Ella Fitzgerald filled the car, soothing him as it always did.

'I like your dad,' she persisted. 'He's always struck me as a fair man.'

'Fair? You've got to be kidding. Try demanding, hard, near-sighted. Except when it comes to his wives, of course. With them, he's a pushover.'

'Do you miss your mum?'

He swallowed the rising bitterness. 'Yeah, you could say that.'

'Do you blame your dad for what happened to her?'

'What do you think?' he snapped, his patience wearing thin. 'What's with the twenty questions anyway?'

She paused, her voice barely rising over the muted jazz. 'It's been a while. I just wanted to get reacquainted, find out what makes you tick.'

'Don't waste your time. This is business, remember?'

If he said it often enough, it might take his mind off her lush curves and the delicate floral perfume that had haunted his senses all evening.

'How could I forget?'

He noted a hint of sadness in her voice. 'About tomorrow—'

'Sorry, Matt. I don't think I can make it. I forgot that the Normanbys want me back to finalise a quote.'

He sighed in relief. 'Rain check?'

'Sure. Why don't you fax me a copy of the engagements you expect me to attend over the next few weeks and I'll slot them into my diary?'

'Good. I like a woman who's organised.'

'You like women period.'

He turned to face her as he stopped the car outside her house. 'Where did that come from?'

He couldn't make out the expression in her eyes as she gazed at him in the dim street lighting. 'Sorry, I must be tired. Goodnight. Let me know your schedule.'

He leaned forward, drawn towards her by some inexplicable force. 'Goodnight, Kara. Pleasant dreams.'

His lips grazed her cheek. He'd have preferred her full lips but she turned her head at the last moment. He could have sworn she muttered 'not likely' as she stepped from the car. He watched her stride up the paved pathway without as much as a glance back over her shoulder. He willed her to look. She didn't and disappointment niggled at his gut. Gunning the engine, he manoeuvred the car away from the kerb, ready for another sleepless night, his dreams once again haunted by her memory.

Kara gave up any pretence at sleep around six and rolled out of bed, rubbing her gritty eyes. The charade with Matt was going to be harder than she thought. Last night had been amazing; he'd held her hand, flashed her intimate smiles and flirted with her for the entire evening. Those three hours had been magical as she caught a glimpse of what it would be like to be Matt Byrne's girlfriend.

Cherished. That was what she'd been. When Matt paid a woman attention, it was like being picked up, cradled and stroked, all warmth and softness. She'd allowed herself to forget who she was for those precious few hours and lapped up the attention.

Her response to his sailing invitation had been reflex. God, she would love to spend the day on an isolated yacht with the man of her dreams. However, reality had set in on the way home and she'd made up that lame excuse about seeing clients. Sadly, he'd been just as eager to get out of it as she had. Then why ask her in the first place? Their situation was becoming more complex by the minute.

After a refreshing shower and quick breakfast, she lay back on the couch to scour the weekend newspapers. She'd barely made it to page three when the doorbell rang. With her pulse accelerating in anticipation, she opened the door.

'Surprise, darling! Time for a cuppa?' Sally bustled through the door, a waft of her signature rose essence left in her wake.

Kara was always glad to see Sal. However, there was no denying that she'd hoped her visitor might be a tall, gorgeous lawyer with flashing blue eyes. 'Sure, Sal. Besides, have I ever said no to your weekend calls when you always bring croissants for brunch? Take a seat and I'll put the kettle on.'

'Seen the papers this morning?' Sally asked as she sat at the table.

'I've just started reading them. Why?'

'No reason. Did you do anything last night?'

'I went out for dinner. Nothing terribly important.'

She could have sworn that Sally snorted. 'Could've fooled me.'

'Pardon?'

'Nothing, dear. Why don't you bring the tea and those crescent-shaped excuses for calories over here and we'll read them together?'

Sally was up to something. Kara knew that twinkle in her eye. It was the same look Sal had given her the other night, after Matt had matched her as his perfect date.

'Whatever you say. Here's your cuppa.'

Glancing over Sal's shoulder at the newspaper, she almost dropped the plate of croissants.

'Will you look at this? Isn't that you and Matt, in the gossip columns, no less?' Sal's wide-eyed innocence didn't fool her for a second.

'Show me that!' She snatched the offending page away as Sal chortled.

Sure enough, there was a colour photo of the two of them at dinner last night, spread over page ten. As if that wasn't bad enough, the accompanying article raved on about Matt's latest 'stunner' and how happy they looked together.

'Great. Just great.' She flung the newspaper back on the table and sat down.

'What's up, dear? If some photographer captured me looking like that, with a man who looks like that, I'd be rapt.'

She saw the confusion in Sal's eyes. How could she begin to explain what she was feeling without disillusioning the woman who had loved and supported her for all these years?

'I just don't like publicity, Sal. Besides, what would they know about my friendship with Matt? They didn't ask us, they just made up what they wanted to.'

Sal reached over and patted her hand. 'I'm glad to hear that you two are friends again. I thought the speed dating might bring you closer. I always thought it was a shame you lost touch, especially after how close you once were.'

Kara had never explained the reason behind her dwindling friendship with Matt. Sal hadn't asked, though she had given her odd looks whenever Kara avoided the topic of the Byrne family.

'Was the speed-dating thing a set-up, Sal?'

The twinkle was back. 'Of course not. You chose each other. How could I complete your forms? Seems like fate to me.'

Kara wrinkled her nose. 'Fate's a four-letter word to me. I hate it. It's turned my life upside-down.'

Sally stood up, walked around the table and hugged her. 'You've been alone for far too long. An attractive girl like you needs a nice young man in her life and I happen to think that Matt Byrne is perfect. What's the harm in going out with him?'

If you only knew. 'Just don't go getting your hopes up. We're going out as friends for a while, nothing more. You'll need to keep that wedding hat under wraps for a bit longer, OK?'

Sal pinched her cheek. 'Too late, darling. It's already out of mothballs. Don't wait too long to set the date, will you?'

She swatted Sal's bottom with the newspaper. 'Go away and leave me alone, you incorrigible old woman!'

'I love you too, sweetheart. Talk to you soon.' With a wave, Sal sailed out the door, croissant in hand.

Kara unrolled the newspaper and spread it on the table. Damn, Matt photographed well. He looked just as delectable in grainy print as he did in the flesh. How could she push him out of her thoughts when he was everywhere she looked?

She didn't look too bad either, thank goodness. If the entire city of Sydney had to see her, at least she looked presentable. They looked happy, with Matt smiling down at her, his arm around her waist and she gazing up at him in adoration. If a picture painted a thousand words, this one was a classic.

Could they rekindle their friendship? Probably, but would she be satisfied with just a friendship? Wasn't that one of the reasons she'd deliberately lost touch, apart from the mortification at being pushed away by him? She'd wanted so much more from the man she'd fallen in love with. What was the point of dredging up old feelings better left forgotten?

As she stared at the picture, Kara knew she was fooling herself. Her feelings for Matt weren't forgotten, just buried. Unfortunately, she feared they would resurface with a little encouragement and posing as his girlfriend might just be the catalyst to set off a disastrous reaction.

'I don't love him. Not any more,' she mumbled, folding the newspaper to hide his grinning image.

However, his mocking smile was imprinted on her mind. She wished that her feelings were as easily folded and tucked away.

CHAPTER SEVEN

IT WAS a perfect summer's day, the cloudless blue sky forming a picturesque backdrop for the stately opera house. Myriad boats dotted Sydney Harbour, people taking advantage of the ideal sailing conditions. Kara leaned back and tilted her face towards the sun, lapping up the rays.

'I hope you're wearing sunscreen.'

She sat up and squinted at Matt behind the wheel. 'Of course I am. I'm not silly, you know.'

'Could've fooled me,' he teased.

She smiled, amazed at how far they had come in such a short space of time. Two months ago, she would have bitten his head off for that remark. She'd been so defensive back then. Now, after many business dinners and chats over coffee, she'd let her guard down. And was enjoying it.

'So where are you taking me, Captain?'

He doffed his cap in a mock salute. 'Wherever m'lady fancies.'

A sliver of anticipation ran down her spine as they sailed under the harbour bridge. 'Why don't you surprise me?'

'I think I can do that.'

He gunned the motor and they sped along, her skin lapping up the refreshing bursts of sea spray. She didn't speak, content to watch him handle the boat with the competency of an expert. He looked striking in white shorts and a navy polo shirt. His long, tanned legs braced his body as the boat picked up speed and she admired his sinewy biceps controlling the wheel. He was a man for all seasons, looking just as good in casual gear as he did in designer suits. She couldn't wait till they dropped anchor. It had been too long since she'd seen him in bathers.

He manoeuvred the boat into a nearby channel and cut the engine. Silence enveloped them as she glanced around. Majestic eucalyptus framed the sandy shore, their verdant foliage in stark contrast to the cerulean ocean. She loved the tributaries off Sydney Harbour, a peaceful haven away from the waterway crowds.

'So, what do you think?'

He opened the refrigerator and removed a bottle of champagne and two chilled glasses.

She stared up at him. 'It's lovely,' she murmured, her eyes fixed on him.

'Thank you.'

She looked away in a hurry, hoping he couldn't read the yearning expression in her eyes. Sal always said she was an open book. She hoped to God that Matt wasn't into reading her genre.

'Here. This should take the edge off.' He handed her a flute of champagne. 'Cheers. To my stunning *girlfriend*.' His smile was intimate, warm, like a caress.

Heat suffused her cheeks as she sipped the amber liquid. The bubbles tickled as they slid down her parched throat. If only she *was* his girlfriend and the day wasn't part of the charade.

'Why did you invite me here?' There. She'd asked the question that had been bugging her all week.

He paused a moment. 'Because I like your company and I thought you might like a day on the harbour.'

'There's no one around, though. It can't be part of our deal.' Too late, she realised she'd spoken aloud.

He swore softly. 'Let's forget the damn deal for today, OK? It's a beautiful day, we're old friends enjoying each other's company; why not leave it at that?'

She shrugged, though her conscience was far from appeased. Too many casual outings in his company without the safety net of their deal would be detrimental to her well-being. 'If you say so.'

'Good. Now that's settled, let's eat.'

She watched him unpack a selection of delicacies and spread them on the deck. As he bent over the picnic basket, she realised just how ravenous she was. And it wasn't for food.

'Hope you're hungry.' He turned a fraction too quickly. She dropped her gaze in record speed but not fast enough. A devilish grin spread over his face. 'See anything you fancy?'

She made a desperate reach for the nearest plate. 'Yeah, the buns look good.'

There was a moment of stunned silence before he burst into laughter. He was joined by a nearby kookaburra in a loud cacophony of raucous chuckles.

A smile tugged at the corners of her mouth as she held her hand up. 'Enough! Time to eat, funny man.'

'Fine. Could you pass me the *buns*—I mean bread, please?'

She ignored his smirk as she filled her plate from the delicious array of food: roast chicken, smoked salmon, sun-dried tomatoes and King Island Brie were a few of her favourites. She wondered if he'd remembered. If lemon meringue pie was dessert, she'd know he had.

They ate in companionable silence, though she was aware of every glance, every gesture, every morsel of food that passed his lips.

'Still hungry?' he asked as he cleared away the empty dishes.

She patted her stomach. 'Not really. That was delicious.'

'What about dessert? It's your favourite.'

He did remember! After all these years. 'Thanks

for doing all this. Lunch was terrific.' She didn't add 'you're terrific', as much as she wanted to.

He sat beside her, sending her heightened senses into overdrive. He smelled delicious, a tempting combination of citrus aftershave, sun and fresh sea air. She inhaled deeply, imprinting the scent on her brain. Whenever she drove past the harbour in future, she wanted to remember this day, this man.

'You have a crumb right there.' He cupped her chin and brushed the corner of her mouth with his thumb.

His feather-light touch sent shivers of excitement shooting from her mouth to her core. An involuntary moan escaped her lips, a soft sound that was deafening in the silence.

His eyes darkened as he continued tracing her lips. 'Hey, I'm not a saint. Unless you stop making sounds like that, I'm going to do something you might regret.'

In response, she leaned towards him, reaching for him. Perhaps she was a little tipsy? It was a fleeting thought as his head descended, blocking out the sunlight.

His kiss tasted of champagne, tart and sweet. Their lips moulded as tongues fused, dancing and teasing.

'That feels so good.' She arched in response to his thumbs stroking her, wanting more. So much more.

'*You* feel so good, Kara,' he whispered against the side of her mouth as his lips trailed along her jaw line to nibble at her ear lobe.

She writhed against him, revelling in the hardness of his body and the feel of his smooth torso. Her hands caressed his muscular back, sliding down to cup his buttocks.

'That's what you wanted for lunch all along, wasn't it?' He flicked her ear with his tongue, setting nerve endings alight throughout her body.

She squeezed his butt. 'I'm not sure. The other buns seemed firmer, crispier.'

He growled and rolled, pinning her beneath him. She smiled at him as her hands continued their leisurely exploration up and down his back.

'You're beautiful.' Matt stared down at Kara, noting her flushed cheeks, her slightly swollen lips, her shining green eyes. He'd wanted her so badly, for so long, that he could hardly believe this was happening.

'What are we doing, Matt?'

The uncertainty of her question was belaid by her wondrous hands. He couldn't think straight. If she kept that up, it would be all over before it began. Pulling away slightly, he rolled onto his side, keeping his arm around her waist. 'Seems pretty obvious to me, sweetheart.'

Her hands stilled. 'I don't want this to be just sex.'

'What do you want it to be?' He ran a finger down her cheek, marvelling at its softness. She felt amazing: soft skin, lush curves, full breasts. God, he could still remember the image of her darkened nipples against that wet white T-shirt all those years ago. It had haunted him ever since.

She stared directly at him. 'I don't know what I want this to be.' She ran her hands through her blonde hair, which shimmered in the sunlight like golden silk. 'I don't want to be just another conquest for you. It would make walking away at the end too difficult.'

Bitterness rose swiftly, dousing him like a bucket of icy water. He dropped his hand. 'Who said you'd have to walk away at the end?'

She tugged her ribbed tank top down as she sat up. 'We both know this is going nowhere. The deal is over in less than four months and you'll happily return to your previous lifestyle. I'm not into casual sex so let's continue the charade and leave it at that.' Her voice had risen several notes, her words piercing him to the core.

'It always comes back to the bloody deal, doesn't it? Is the money that important to you?' He kept his voice deliberately low. He swore he saw a glitter of tears in her eyes before she turned away.

'Yes, it is.'

Those three little words hurt. Short, sharp, deep.

She sure didn't mince words and he was having a hard time accepting them. He shook his head, trying to clear his thoughts.

'I need to cool off.' He stripped quickly and dived into the water, embracing the icy chill and striking out for the shore.

Kara stared at the figure freestyling away from the boat. She allowed the tears to flow, wishing she hadn't started questioning him. God, what a mess. It was a revelation to find that Matt wanted her, his passion matching her own. After the kiss on their first 'date', witnessed by Steve, he hadn't come near her. Sure, he gave her an affectionate peck in front of colleagues and at the end of their dates, but that was it.

Not that she hadn't practically begged for it today. It must be the sun. That was it, she had heat stroke.

Leaning against the rail and watching him swim away, she knew the only heat stroke she had was fired by Matt. Even now, warmth seeped through her body at the memory of his lips, his hands. She'd been on fire, wanting him with a passion that frightened her in its intensity.

Then why resist?

Fear, pure and simple. At least she'd been partly honest with him. She didn't want to become just another woman he'd bedded. She wanted more. Heck, she wanted it all. She wanted to hear him say that the deal was over, that he loved her so much that he wanted her to be his girlfriend for real, that she wasn't just another acquisition to him.

However, he hadn't said any of those things. She knew he loved women and that was all she was to him, a woman who had made it more than clear she fancied him. Why wouldn't he take advantage of an opportunity like that? Thank goodness she'd come to her senses and brought up the deal.

Once again, she'd used the money as a tangible barrier against heartache. As long as he thought she was only doing this for the money, she would be safe. Having Matt as a friend she could handle. Having Matt as a lover, as someone she loved, was too much. Lord, it was going to be a long four months till their deal was completed.

OK, the sailing day hadn't been one of Matt's better ideas. He didn't know what devil had possessed him to invite the sexiest woman alive to spend the day with him on his yacht. Funny, ever since their first dinner engagement, he'd wanted her alone with him on his yacht. He'd even asked her to go sailing that first night, though she'd thankfully reneged on it.

But two months later he'd done it again. He'd known he wouldn't be able to keep his hands off her yet he'd asked her anyway. It had been hard enough to act the gentleman over their last few dinner dates.

If they hadn't been surrounded by his colleagues, he'd have jumped her over the table a long time ago. So what hope did he have against his rising libido when confined aboard his yacht with a stunner like Kara?

Zilch. He'd replayed that sizzling look she'd given him over and over in his mind, the one that had practically begged him to kiss her. It had been heaven, feeling her soft and pliant beneath him, returning his passion. He'd imagined it so many times, fantasising what it would be like to have her ready for him, moaning his name…

He thumped his desk in frustration. Damn this stupid deal. If it wasn't for the money, he could have developed feelings for Kara. However, one gold-digger in the family at a time was more than enough. Lorna, his latest stepmother, was a real piece of work and lord help him if Kara was anything like her.

He needed to get a grip! Unfortunately, the only person he wanted to grip at this moment was his dad, right around his neck. If it wasn't for his father's ridiculous stipulations regarding being made a partner, he wouldn't have concocted this stupid deal in the first place.

And you wouldn't have run into Kara again. He sighed, shuffling contracts on his desk. Always a double-edged sword. His business dealings were full of them. It was his job to make the deals clearer for his clients. Why couldn't he apply the same rules to his personal life?

A knock on the door interrupted his musings.

'Come in.'

'Wondering if you had a minute, Matt.'

His father strode into his office. Matt hoped that he looked as good as Jeff Byrne at fifty-eight: thick, peppery hair, unlined skin and a vitality that glowed from his blue eyes. No wonder women found him attractive. He wondered if his mum had seen their covetous looks. Was that one of the things that had driven her away?

'Sure. What can I do for you?' He hated the fact that he couldn't call his father 'Dad' in the office. He also wished that just once he would call him 'son' rather than Matt.

'The firm is holding a corporate weekend away. It's in a couple of weeks, so you can give Kara plenty of notice.'

Oh-oh. Matt cleared his throat. 'I'll see what I can do, though Kara is a busy woman. She has a business of her own, you know. She mightn't be free.'

His father waved his hand in the air like a magician. 'Nonsense. Lovely woman, Kara. You've done well there, son. I'm sure she'd love to come away with us. I hear her business isn't doing so great, so she'll probably have the time. Perhaps you can give her some advice?'

He was speechless. His father had actually called him 'son'. And what was that stuff he'd said about Kara's business? Was that why she needed the money?

'Anyway, I'll email the details to you. Don't forget to tell Kara I said hello.' His father paused at the doorway. 'I'm proud of you, son.'

He hadn't imagined it. His dad had called him 'son' again. Matt sat back in his leather-backed chair and exhaled. He'd waited a long time to hear those words from his father. Then why did he feel as if it was a hollow victory? He hated deceiving his dad but the deal was the only way to make his father take him seriously. If today was any indication, he was succeeding. But at what cost? And to whom? The sooner he sorted this mess out, the better. His dad deserved better. So did Kara.

But what about the money? And why is her business in trouble? Is she just using you, like all the rest?

Twirling his pen absent-mindedly, he stared at his calendar. A couple of weeks, huh? He resolved to discuss the deal with her over the weekend away. If the money was that important, he would give it to her. He just wanted their relationship to be obligation-free. No more deals.

What if she doesn't want you without the money?

His heart constricted at the thought. After all,

she'd made it clear right from the start that she didn't want anything to do with him. Maybe she *was* only doing this for the money? He resolved there was only one way to find out. As he reached towards the phone to call her, it rang.

He picked up. 'Matt Byrne speaking.'

'Byrne, you old dog. Been holding out on me. What's all this about you bringing the fair Kara to our weekend away?'

'What do you want, Saunders? I'm busy.'

He hadn't spoken to his best friend Luke Saunders in a few weeks, despite the fact they worked for the same law firm. Luke's criminal caseload meant that the two rarely crossed paths these days.

'I bet you're too busy! You seem to have your hands pretty full...' His mate's voice trailed off in a snigger.

'Cut the crap. I've been working long hours on a few copyright cases. And yes, I've been seeing a bit of Kara, not that it's any of your business.'

Luke guffawed. 'Touched a nerve? Not like you to get all serious about one woman. What gives?'

He wished he could divulge his secret to his friend. Unfortunately, Luke wasn't renowned for his tact. 'Can't a leopard change its spots? I happen to like Kara. A lot.'

There was a definite snort from the other end of the line. 'You? Change spots? You'd need to change species. Are you telling me our carousing days are over?'

'You got it, buddy. You're on your own.'

'But my little black book is overflowing. Can't I tempt you with a Tiffany or an Alannah? Remember the good ol' days?'

'I really need to get back to work. How about I meet you for a drink after work?'

'I suppose.' Luke sighed. 'Wimp.'

Matt chuckled. 'Just think. All the more ladies for you, my friend.'

'Whatever.'

'See you at the local around seven. Bye.'

He stared at the phone, wondering if he should call Kara. Luke's call had distracted him and he wanted to be focused when he invited her away for the weekend. They hadn't spoken much since the debacle on his yacht and he had an inkling that spending a whole weekend in the role of his girlfriend wasn't going to appeal to her a bit.

He would break it to her gently. Flowers, wine, chocolates, then hit her with it? Yeah, subtle as a sledgehammer. How about a formal printed invitation? No, that would definitely scare her away. He needed to tread carefully for her to accept. Tapping his pen on a stack of paperwork, he resolved one thing. He had to ask her in person. The phone wouldn't suffice for something as important as this.

It wasn't like him to be low on confidence. This stupid deal had him on edge. He wished he could be himself with Kara and woo her properly, not with some half-hearted lines while play-acting their roles. Suddenly, it came to him. That was it! He'd been playing a role, not just for the benefit of his father but for Kara also. Why not try being himself? She'd liked him all those years ago, why not try to recapture some of that old magic and see what happened? What did he have to lose?

Byrne, you're a genius.

Then why did he feel like the kid standing in the corner of the classroom wearing a pointy hat with a big D on the front?

CHAPTER EIGHT

KARA sank into the warm water and breathed a sigh of relief. The lavender-scented mist enveloped her in a fragrant cloud, helping her mind to relax. She closed her eyes, shutting out the flickering images of the candles she'd lit. What a week. Thank goodness she'd ignored Olivia's persistent invitation to go out dancing tonight and followed her instincts. A hot bath, a soppy movie and a tub of her favourite strawberry ice cream were all she craved tonight.

Speaking of cravings...a vivid image of Matt popped into her head, blotting out all relaxing thoughts. She'd managed to push him to the far recesses of her mind all week, throwing herself into work. The Normanbys had been suitably impressed, even the old battleaxe. However, during her quieter moments like now, his image would arise, throwing her into chaos once again.

Ever since that hot session on the boat a few weeks ago, her imagination had shifted into overdrive. She'd woken several nights in a row, sweaty and dishevelled from the most erotic dreams involving Matt. Thank goodness he hadn't called for over a week. It was hard enough to talk to him on the phone. How the heck was she going to keep her cool, face to face?

He'd been polite yet withdrawn on the phone, the few times they had spoken. They had exchanged pleasantries but that was about it. She felt he'd been calling out of obligation rather than any burning need to see how she was. She'd even wondered if he'd been seeing anyone else but had quickly squashed that thought; he wanted the partnership in his dad's firm too much to jeopardise it now. After all, he wouldn't have taken the ludicrous deal this far if he didn't want it so badly. Only three months left and she would be free...

Free to do what? Return to scanning the social pages for snippets of his exciting life? Return to turning a pale shade of green at the latest woman in his life?

She needed to get a life. Fast. Perhaps she would enlist Sal's help after all.

'I must be getting desperate,' she murmured, sinking beneath the water. It didn't help. Nothing could wash away the doldrums tonight. Only one thing could lift her spirits but she needed to dry off, open the freezer and grab a spoon before she could try it. Thank God for ice cream, a girl's best friend.

After moisturising, towel-drying her hair and slipping into her piggy pyjamas, she was ready. Armed with a tub of luxury ice cream and her favourite DVD, she sank into the soft leather cushions.

'Come on, Leonardo, make my day.'

As she hit the play button, the doorbell rang.

'Damn,' she mumbled, wondering momentarily if it was too late to turn off the lights and pretend she wasn't home.

No such luck. The doorbell rang again, louder and more insistent this time.

'I'm coming. Hold your horses.'

She opened the door a fraction and peeked around it.

'Hi. Can I come in?'

It was like a recurring nightmare. Whenever she thought about Matt for more than five seconds, he materialised. And she was wearing pig pyjamas, for God's sake!

'Uh…I'm kind of busy at the moment.' It sounded lame and she knew it.

'Promise I won't stay long. I just have to ask you something.' His expression melted her heart: soft, ca-joling, little-boy-lost.

Her curiosity was piqued. 'Just for a minute, OK?'

A warm smile lit up his face. 'Thanks.' He stared at her for what seemed like an eternity. 'Kara? Are you going to let me in?'

She giggled, wishing she'd opted for slinky satin

rather than practical cotton tonight. 'Oh, yeah. Just watch out for the animals.'

'The anim…' He stopped mid-sentence as she unchained the door, a grin slowly spreading across his handsome face.

'If you make one wisecrack about my porcine friends, you're out of here,' she threatened, struggling to keep the laughter out of her voice.

As he looked her up and down and his smile turned to a smirk, she brandished the spoon like a sword. 'I mean it!'

He held his hands up in surrender. 'Don't worry. You won't hear a squeal—uh, I mean, a peep out of me.'

He joined in her laughter and followed her into the lounge room.

'I'm glad you were in. I need to discuss something with you.' He moved around the room, his pacing giving her the impression that he was just as ill at ease as she was.

'OK. Take a seat. Would you like a drink?'

'Coffee would be great.' He picked up the DVD cover and chuckled. 'Nothing like a good chick flick, huh?'

She smiled. 'And what would you know about chick flicks? I thought you'd be an action-movie type.'

He shook his head. 'Just shows you don't know

me very well. I happen to like soppy stuff. I'm a big softy at heart.'

Kara picked up the tub of ice cream she'd been about to devour and headed towards the kitchen. 'You? A softy? Give me a break!'

She busied herself making the coffee, wondering at the silence. When she returned to the lounge room, she found him studying the photos on the marble mantelpiece.

'You must miss them a lot,' he murmured, indicating the photos of her parents.

'Uh-huh. I can't believe it's been so long since the accident.'

He came and sat beside her on the couch. 'The jerk that killed them is probably out on the streets by now.' He sipped his coffee. 'The law stinks when it comes to drunk drivers. I'm glad I don't have to defend them. I just couldn't do it, job or not.'

Kara didn't want to dwell on her parents' death or the drunk who had killed them, using his vehicle as a lethal weapon. She'd dealt with her anger and had moved on, though it didn't stop the pain.

She stared at Matt over the rim of her mug. He looked tired, the lines around his mouth more pronounced and a hint of dark rings under his eyes. He was still gut-wrenchingly sexy, despite the obvious signs of fatigue.

'What did you want to talk about?' Her curiosity

increased as he reached into his pocket and handed her a gilt-edged envelope.

'Here. I thought you might like this.'

She opened the envelope. A small, ornate key slid onto her palm. There was no accompanying instructions. She glanced up, unable to fathom the intensity of his stare. 'OK, I give up. What's this all about?'

'Remember that summer when we used to hang out at the boat shed and I found your diary key?'

How could she forget? It had been the summer when she'd fallen in love with him and her diary had held all her secret longings. 'Yeah, I remember,' she answered cautiously, wondering where this was leading.

'Well, you freaked out and demanded I give you back the key. I did, though I wanted to find out what made you tick.'

She raised an eyebrow. 'And?'

'When we met at the Blue Lounge, you wanted to know what made me tick. This key is giving you the opportunity to find out.'

She noted the expectant look on his face, the mischievous glint in his eyes. He was up to something. Placing the key on the glass-topped coffee-table, she decided to call his bluff. 'You're too complex for me, Matt Byrne. I've given up trying to work you out.'

He edged towards her, his evocative masculine

scent wrapping her in a cloak of familiarity. 'Aren't you up for the challenge?'

He'd done it again. Drawing on their memories, using them as a persuasive tool. He knew she'd never backed away from a challenge, ever. And she wasn't about to blemish her record now.

'OK, mister. You're on. Tell me what the key fits.'

He picked up the key and dangled it in front of her. 'Not so quick. Are you free the weekend after next?'

'Maybe. Depends who's asking,' she teased, snatching the key out of his hand and twirling it on her finger.

He chuckled, a low, throaty sound that never failed to make her feel warm, safe, secure. 'Well, if you're free, the firm is having a weekend away. Sort of an annual retreat thing. Spouses are invited, so I was wondering if you'd like to come.'

He reached out and stilled her hand. The key plopped onto the couch and lay between them, gleaming against the cream cushions. At his touch, her pulse accelerated, her breathing becoming shallow. Desire slammed through her, all the fantasies of the last few weeks focusing on this man, this moment. She tried to extricate her hand, but he wouldn't let go. He intertwined his fingers with hers, using his thumb to circle her palm.

'What about the key?' she asked, barely able to

think straight as wave after wave of pleasurable sensation washed over her.

'That's part of the deal. If you come away with me, you get to use the key and find out all about me.' He stared at her, bold, daring.

'Not another damn deal,' she murmured, unable to tear her gaze away from the challenge behind his stare.

He cursed softly. 'Poor choice of words, sweetheart. This weekend means a lot to me. I'm hoping we can sort out a few things and set the record straight.' He reached across and cupped her cheek.

She could scarcely breathe. It wasn't just his touch; the hint of vulnerability mingled with boyish charm undid her completely. 'I'll come with you,' she managed to squeak out, willing him to kiss her.

'That's great.' He beamed, his smile illuminating the room better than the down-lights. 'I'm looking forward to it.'

She leaned towards him, parting her lips in anticipation. 'Me too.'

He stared at her for an interminable second before standing up in one swift, abrupt movement. 'Thanks for the coffee. I'll give you all the details once I have them.'

She took a deep breath and exhaled, trying to pull herself together. Once again, she'd practically thrown herself at him. It was becoming a habit, one she desperately needed to break if her sanity was to remain intact. Just tell that to her body.

'Thanks for the invitation.' She bent down and picked up the key. 'I look forward to using this. Unlocking your secrets is going to be fun.'

'I'll hold you to that.' He placed a chaste kiss on her cheek, winked and walked away. She stared after him, admiring the view.

'Goodnight, Matt.'

A strange, grunting sound was his response.

'If that was an oink, you're in trouble!'

He turned at the front door. 'And what are you going to do about it, Miss Piggy?'

He ducked the flying cushion she flung at him. 'I'd better go. I've got to be up early tomorrow, to head off to work and bring home the bacon.'

'Get out! I said no pig jokes.'

He held his hands up in surrender. 'OK, OK. Personally, I think they're kind of cute…or is that the woman wearing them?'

Her laughter died as he blew her a kiss and shut the door behind him. So much for cool. So much for detachment. In less than half an hour, he'd shattered her carefully erected barriers yet again. Her infatuation hadn't dimmed at all. If anything, he had fanned the flames of her desire and it threatened to burn like an out-of-control inferno.

Tonight had been different. She'd sensed it the

moment he came in. He'd been less confident, more open. In fact, he'd been the Matt of old, the guy she knew all those years ago. *The guy you loved.* She pushed the thought aside, though it refused to be ignored. Once it had insinuated its way into her consciousness, she couldn't refute it.

So what if she'd loved him? It was over. Loved. Past tense.

As she unclenched her fist and looked at the small key in her palm, her stomach churned. Was she playing with fire? Did she really want to get burned again? She flipped the key over and over, hoping for an answer. What did it unlock? Whatever it was, she hoped it wasn't a Pandora's box.

Matt revved the engine of his car and slid away from the kerb. He was tightly wound, like a cobra ready to uncoil and strike. He'd barely made it out of Kara's apartment, resolutions intact. It had taken every ounce of his limited will-power to walk away from her. She'd wanted his kiss, he was sure of it. And he'd resisted, despite the fact he'd wanted her the minute she'd opened the front door and he'd seen those cutesy pyjamas.

Damn, had his tastes changed! He loved lingerie on women and the smooth, sexy feel of satin beneath his hands, yet one glimpse of Kara in those cotton

PJs and he'd been almost salivating. How could pigs be sexy? He must be losing his mind!

However, he knew it had nothing to do with the sleepwear and everything to do with the woman wearing it. It wasn't enough he'd slept poorly for the last few weeks since their passionate interlude on the yacht. Now he had to contend with the tantalising image of her bending forward, giving him a glimpse of full breasts beneath the cotton.

He must be a sadist. Why else would he inflict this sort of torture on himself? He couldn't get enough of her yet all he seemed to do was push her away. The weekend away would be different. Perhaps give them a chance to complete what they had started on the yacht? With no strings attached, of course, just the way he liked it.

He could never contemplate the L word, especially with Kara. He had no intention of falling for a woman who viewed money as a prerequisite to spending time with him, not that he'd thought much about the cash the last few times they'd been together. He'd been too caught up in her spell to think straight let alone ponder her reasons for asking such a steep price.

So she'd put paid to his wandering eye temporarily. Thank goodness he was nothing like his father. Even though Jeff Byrne said that admiring women was like appreciating fine art, Matt knew it must have caused his mother grief. Why else would she have abandoned him when he was only six years old, leaving him with a workaholic father who had remarried his secretary in just over a year?

Matt wasn't stupid. He'd put two and two together at an early age, throwing tantrums when his father used to bring home 'Aunty Denise' only a few months after his mum had left. When she'd moved in, he'd been devastated and refused to acknowledge her as his stepmother. Surprisingly, Denise had stayed married to his dad for twenty years and he'd grown to like her. It had come as a shock when she'd left his father, though yet again his dad had remarried as soon as the divorce came through. Enter Lorna, wife number three and the biggest gold-digger of them all. How could his father be that gullible?

Matt thumped the steering wheel, registering shock at the clarity of his thoughts. How could he accuse his dad of being foolish with Lorna when he was just as bad where Kara was concerned? Sure, she found him attractive, but the money was an integral part of that attraction. She'd even said as much. No money, no deal.

He shook his head as he parked the car and entered the apartment. There was no way he would let any woman sink her greedy claws into him. Even if she was the woman who could fulfil every one of his fantasies and leave him hankering for more.

* * *

Kara zipped her overnight bag, wishing she could shut down the million rampaging butterflies in her stomach just as easily. She glanced around the bedroom, checking that she hadn't left any last-minute items lying around. Not that she could tell. There was a multitude of outfits strewn on the bed in higgledy-piggledy disarray, with underwear thrown in for good measure. She'd been through her wardrobe a hundred times, selecting and disregarding clothes at random.

This weekend was important and she needed to present a confident front. Matt's invitation had intrigued her and his mysterious key had been burning a hole in her purse for the last two weeks. He certainly knew how to push her buttons. Life was never dull with Matt around; he was vibrant, fun-loving, addictive. Yes, he was definitely the latter. She craved him all the time, yearning for a word, a smile, a touch, her next fix.

A knock interrupted her thoughts. Grabbing her bag, she headed for the door, her pulse beating a staccato rhythm in anticipation.

'Hi, gorgeous. Ready to go?' Matt grinned at her, a reassuring warmth radiating from his blue eyes.

'Ready as I'll ever be,' she replied, trying not to stare. He looked incredible, clad in snug jeans, a white T-shirt that hugged his muscular torso and a black leather jacket.

'Let's hit the road, then. It's a two-hour drive to

King River and we don't want to miss dinner tonight. I hear the food at this place is gourmet all the way.'

She nodded, distracted by the sight of his denim-clad butt bending over to pick up her overnight bag. When she didn't answer, he looked up.

'Oh-oh. Looks like you're craving buns again.'

She blushed, feeling the heat sweeping into her cheeks. Tucking a stray strand of hair behind her ear, she fumbled for an excuse. 'I—I was just checking out the label. Looks like a pair I once owned.'

The corners of his mouth twitched. 'Really?' He hoisted her bag over his shoulder with apparent ease and offered her his hand. 'If you're lucky, you can take a closer look later.'

She ignored his hand, locked the door and strode towards the car. His laughter taunted her, doing little to still her galloping heart. If he only knew how good his offer sounded.

They chatted for the entire journey, small talk mostly. However, she was dying to ask him one vital question that had been bugging her since she'd accepted his invitation. She waited till the homestead came into view, knowing she couldn't avoid it any longer.

'What a beautiful place. How did you find it?'

He shrugged. 'Dad stayed here once. It has great conference facilities, not to mention the usual recreation stuff like a heated indoor pool, tennis, billiards. Though I think it was the food that sucked him in. He raved about it for a month afterwards.'

'Sounds great.' She scanned the landscape, noting the towering eucalyptus, the gently undulating hills and the lush paddocks that stretched for miles. 'How many does it sleep?' There, she'd finally asked the million-dollar question.

She sensed Matt look across. 'Ten couples. I think that's how many Dad's booked for.'

She fidgeted with her sleeve, plucking nervously at an imaginary thread. 'About the sleeping arrangements—'

'Don't worry about it,' he interrupted. 'We'll have to share a room and a bed for appearance' sake but I think I can control myself. What about you?'

A picture of the two of them entwined in bed rose before her eyes. She blinked, wishing her imagination would calm down. 'No problems here. I just wanted to make it clear from the start. You know, to avoid any uncomfortable situations.'

He chuckled. 'Hey, if you're that concerned, we can always sleep top to tail.'

'But that wouldn't stop…' she trailed off, horrified at what she'd been about to say.

'Gotcha!'

She whacked him on the arm as he stopped the car on the gravel driveway.

He rubbed his arm and turned to face her. 'Lady, you pack a powerful punch.'

'That's nothing. Wait till you see what I have planned if you really get out of line!'

His eyes glimmered in the fading light as the sun set around them in a staggering array of muted colour. 'Promises, promises,' he murmured, reaching out and cupping her chin.

She stared, transfixed. There was no pulling away, even if she wanted to. 'Shouldn't we go inside?'

'Eventually.'

As he leaned towards her, there was a loud honking of a horn and they jerked apart like two teenagers caught necking. A sporty red convertible pulled up next to them and the driver's window slid down.

'Hey, you two. Great timing, though what are you doing out here in the car? Thought you'd be *unpacking* by now.' Luke Saunders winked at her. She'd met him several times and loved his cheeky sense of humour.

'Good idea,' Matt mumbled, though it sounded as though it was the last thing he wanted to do.

With a wave, Luke pulled away and parked near by.

'He's a nice guy,' she volunteered, confused by Matt's continuing silence.

'Think so?'

She couldn't fathom his sudden reluctance to go

in, especially considering their almost-kiss minutes ago. 'What's up?'

To her surprise, he reached over and grabbed her hand. 'I really appreciate you doing this for me, Kara. I know that posing as my girlfriend for a professional dinner is a helluva lot different from doing it for a whole weekend. I just hope you're still talking to me by the end of it.'

His behaviour was making her increasingly nervous. 'Why wouldn't I be? Is there something you're not telling me?'

He shook his head. 'No, though a lot of people are going to assume we're closer than close after this weekend, including my father. I just wanted to warn you, that's all.'

She squeezed his hand. 'Don't worry. I'll be the model girlfriend, you'll see. A deal's a deal, remember?'

A sad look passed over his face as he dropped her hand. 'Yeah, it is. Time to face the music, I guess.'

There was little time to say anything else, as Luke opened her door. 'Need a hand?'

She smiled, uncertainty rendering her speechless. What the hell was she doing, playing at a role she'd coveted her entire life? Surely Matt's dad and his closest colleagues would work out that she was a phoney over the weekend? And if so, what would that do to his chances of being made a partner, and in turn, what would happen to Sally's business? Not to mention her own? The sooner she wrapped up the DATY for Sal, the sooner she could focus her attentions on saving Inner Sanctum.

Half listening to the men talk as they climbed the porch steps, she heard a squeal of tyres. They turned in time to see a bright yellow convertible screech to a halt, gravel flying in its wake. The car had barely stopped when a statuesque brunette unfolded her long legs from behind the wheel and stepped out.

'Great. There's my date now.'

Matt stared at the woman, his tanned face paling as he turned to Luke. 'You invited Miranda? What gives?'

Luke winked. 'She's the love of my life. At least for this week.'

'You're crazy, you know that?' She watched Matt clench and unclench his fists several times, tension evident in the taut set of his shoulders.

'Do you know her?' Kara ventured, not liking the vibes she was picking up.

Matt turned to her then, as if noticing her for the first time. 'Yeah, you could say that.'

He ran his fingers through his hair, sending spikes in every direction. 'We'll see you inside,' he called out to Luke, who was already lost in a clinch with the voluptuous Miranda.

He took her elbow and guided her up the remaining steps, a look of disgust on his face.

'Is she an ex-girlfriend?'

He nodded. 'She's a girl and she's an ex, but she sure isn't a friend. I can't believe Luke's hooked up with her. Can we change the subject now?'

A swift stab of jealousy pierced her gut. 'Whatever, but for someone who isn't a friend, you sure seem to be annoyed about something.'

'Leave it,' he muttered as he pushed open the heavy oak door. 'What's happened in the past stays in the past. Let's just hope Mandy remembers that rule.'

Mandy. The pet name didn't assuage her jealousy, not one little bit. She tried to keep the bitterness out of her voice. 'What's the matter? I thought you'd love having more than one woman fawning all over you.'

'Bitchiness isn't flattering.'

'Neither is purchasing and parading a token girlfriend for the benefit of furthering one's career.'

Colour drained from his face for the second time in less than five minutes. She stepped back involuntarily, knowing she'd gone too far.

'I'm going to unpack. Our room is number eight. If you choose to join me, fine. If not, I don't give a damn any more.' He threw her the car keys and she caught them, purely a reflex action. 'It's your call. Either way, I don't care.'

She watched him stride away, tears stinging her eyes. She wanted him to care, dammit! She wanted him to care as much as she did…and more. What the hell was she going to do now?

CHAPTER NINE

MATT unlocked the door and strode into the room, barely noticing his surroundings. He couldn't believe that his plans were ruined already. So much for romancing the woman of his dreams this weekend. Right now, he didn't know if she would stay or leave.

He was a realist and thought she would choose the latter. He'd lost his cool back there but if it was one thing he couldn't stand, it was jealousy. He'd seen his father's string of gold-diggers use it too many times to get what they wanted. Sure, his behaviour when Miranda had arrived hadn't been anything to write home about, but why the interrogation?

Maybe she cares more than you think. The thought popped into his head, offering small comfort. Another thought closely followed. For a man who couldn't harbour jealousy, the green-eyed monster had certainly stirred to life when he'd heard Steve Rockwell was Kara's ex. And what had he done about it? He'd wanted to punch the offender right in the nose. So why was he judging her before giving her a chance? God, for a smart lawyer, he was stupid sometimes.

Eager to straighten things out, he wrenched open the door and barged out, almost colliding with Kara.

'Can I come in?' She spoke softly, uncertainty etched across her face.

Relief flooded him as he stepped aside, resisting the temptation to sweep her into his arms and carry her to the bed. 'Sure. Let me take your bag.'

Her gaze darted around the room before coming to rest on the huge four-poster bed that dominated it. 'This is lovely,' she murmured.

He looked around as if seeing it for the first time, noticing the polished floorboards, the burgundy rugs and the matching quilt on the bed. He stared at the king-size bed and willed his mind not to fantasise. It didn't work and he was hard within a second.

Turning his attention back to Kara didn't help either. She was clad in tight camel trousers and a figure-hugging khaki jumper, her lips highlighted with gloss and her cat-like eyes focused on him, and the sight of her tempted him to fulfil every thought that had just flashed through his mind.

'I'm sorry about before.' The words tumbled out in a rush before he could think.

A smile tugged at the corners of her mouth. 'Matt Byrne apologising? That's got to be a first.'

He shrugged, his confidence somewhat restored by the cheeky grin on her face. 'I call it as I see it.'

'Are you saying that you behaved abominably and

that you'd really like me to stay?' She batted her eyelashes like an experienced flirt.

'Don't push it, lady!' he growled, striding across the room. He enveloped her in a hug, savouring the feel of her soft curves pressed against him. Her subtle floral perfume wrapped around him as he inhaled, allowing it to infuse his senses. The signature scent triggered memories of her eighteenth birthday, when he'd pushed her away. This weekend he wouldn't be so foolish.

She wriggled in his arms. 'So when do I get to use the key?'

'Key? What key?' He schooled his features into a mask of indifference, which was no mean feat considering he wanted to split his sides laughing at the look of consternation on her face.

She pulled away and folded her arms. The defensive gesture drew his attention to her full breasts, pushed higher by the action. The blood roared through his veins as he yearned to cup their weight in his hands, to caress, to stroke, to taste…

'Don't play coy with me, Matthew Byrne. That mysterious key is what brought me here this weekend and you know it.'

He clutched his heart. 'And I thought it was my devastating charm that led you here. You sure know how to wound a guy.'

She dropped her hands onto her hips. That jumper

was a knockout, accentuating every curve and enhancing the intense green of her eyes. 'If you're toying with me, there certainly will be some wounding going on this weekend and it won't just be to your ego.' Her glance travelled downwards and focused on his groin region as her knee lifted in a mock kick.

'Ouch!' He grimaced. 'Don't even think about it.' He noticed her gaze stayed riveted, even as he spoke. 'Besides, I can think of much more pleasurable pursuits if you're heading in that general direction.'

Her eyes widened as a blush stained her cheeks. 'I'm going to unpack.' She whirled around and bent to unzip her bag.

'What about the key?' he asked, eager to continue their jousting and see where it might lead.

'I'm sure you'll reveal its use in good time,' she flung over her shoulder. 'Right now, I'm going to take a shower and get ready for dinner.'

'That's not all I might reveal!'

She slammed the bathroom door on his laughter.

Dinner was a nightmare. Kara thought it had been hard to pose as Matt's girlfriend on their previous outings but she'd seen nothing yet. Surrounded by his closest work colleagues, his friends, not to mention his father, she was way out of her depth. Posing in front of business acquaintances had been a lot easier. Her face ached from smiling, her heart ached from the deception. Jeff Byrne treated her like a long-lost daughter, parading her proudly for his employees. She could almost have carried it off if it wasn't for Matt's burning stare following her every move.

Her body throbbed with awareness, whether he was at her side or across the room. Every glance, every caress, every smile drove her closer to the brink of losing control. How could she share a room with this man, let alone a bed, and keep it strictly platonic?

As the evening wound down to a close, her nerves stretched to breaking point. The infamous Miranda, who had managed to wind every man present around her little finger, chose this time to approach her.

'Hi. You must be Kara. I'm Miranda.' She held out a perfectly manicured hand.

Kara had expected a cold grip to match the iceprincess façade, yet her hand was surprisingly warm. 'Nice to meet you.'

'So you're Matt's latest girlfriend?'

'Yes. And he's told me all about you.' She kept the rancour out of her voice, wondering if she would burn in hell for the little white lie.

'He has?' Miranda's plucked eyebrows shot up. 'I hope there's no hard feelings, then. He hasn't spoken to me since we split up. You know, bad karma and all that.'

She watched the brunette fidget with the neckline of her black silk dress, which threatened to plunge lower with every passing second. Suddenly she pitied her, knowing what it was like to be unloved and unwanted by a man like Matt.

'Don't worry about it. I'm sure you two will talk again, especially now you're seeing his best friend.'

Miranda smiled, showing a staggering display of capped teeth gleaming in the lamplight. 'You're really nice. I'm so glad Matt's chosen you to settle down with.'

Kara chuckled, trying to ignore the increased tempo of her heartbeat. 'Who told you that?'

'Luke, of course. Those two are practically joined at the hip and he says that Matt's gaga over you. He's never seen him like this over anybody.'

Before Kara could answer, Jeff joined them.

'Ah, just my luck to be surrounded by the two most beautiful women in the room. Enjoying yourselves, ladies?'

Kara nodded, happy for Miranda to launch into conversation with him while she sought out Matt. She spotted him near the snooker table, deep in conversation with Luke. Her heart contracted as she considered what Miranda had told her.

Was Luke's estimation accurate? Did Matt care for her or was he just a damn good actor? Luke worked in the firm and was obviously on good terms with

Jeff, so wouldn't Matt need to convince him of their relationship in the hope it would bolster his chances of a partnership with his dad? That had to be it. It was the only logical explanation and it hurt more than she cared to admit. For one brief, ecstatic minute, she wanted to believe that he loved her, before reality set in.

She excused herself and left the room, eager to find a quiet spot to compose her thoughts. Their room was no good, for that was the first place Matt would search for her. Almost without thinking, she headed for the pool house, which was linked to the main house by a long glass-enclosed corridor. Several chaise longues surrounded the sparkling clear pool, which would have challenged any Olympic swimmer. The humid air clung to her skin, warm enough for her to lie back on one of the chairs and close her eyes.

If dinner had been a nightmare, the remainder of the night was going to be sheer hell. She'd used every excuse in the book to convince herself that she didn't love Matt: rich, successful lawyers weren't her type, he was a playboy who would love her and leave her, his lifestyle demanded the perfect image and she only provided that for other people as part of her business.

Not to mention the biggest excuse, the fact she'd offered herself to him once before and he'd rejected her. Every reason was valid yet she wasn't convinced. She loved him, pure and simple. She'd finally realised it that night at her place when he'd invited her to accompany him on this weekend.

It hadn't been one particular thing he'd said or done. She'd just known, as soon as he left, that her life was empty without him. She loved him, had probably always loved him. So what the hell was she going to do when he slipped into bed beside her tonight? And worse, when he slipped out of her life at the conclusion of their deal?

She wasn't stupid. She'd seen the evidence of his desire earlier that afternoon and it hadn't been the first time. Matt hadn't hid the fact that he found her sexually appealing since she'd signed the stupid deal. So what was new? Didn't he find all women appealing? He probably thought it was perfectly natural that sex was part of the deal. After all, she seriously doubted that any woman had been silly enough to knock him back in the past. Well, she was going to be the first. She had to be, if she was going to survive the next few months with her heart intact.

A sudden splash interrupted her thoughts and she looked towards the pool but couldn't see anyone. Seconds ticked by. Whoever was underwater could hold their breath for longer than she could. Just as she was starting to panic, Matt hoisted himself out of the pool before her eyes.

Her throat constricted as she watched water droplets sluice down his magnificently toned body and fall in gentle plops onto the tiles. She'd caught a glimpse of his body that day on the yacht, but hadn't been in any frame of mind to register its splendour. Tonight she had all the time in the world to appreciate his broad shoulders, washboard abs and lean, muscular legs. He had the body of an athlete, not an ounce of extra weight gracing his torso.

He strolled towards her, wearing nothing but the briefest of black bathers and a smile.

'Fancy a dip?' he murmured, holding out his hand.

She stared at him, mesmerised by the hunger in his eyes, which had darkened to the colour of midnight. 'I—I haven't brought a swimsuit,' she stammered, placing her hand tentatively in his.

'So?' The whispered word hung between them, intensifying the moment tenfold.

The cloying humidity plucked at her dress and she had an urge to tear it off as he pulled her towards him, crushing her against his body.

Kara moaned as his mouth sought hers. She parted her lips and welcomed his devouring kiss, all thoughts of resistance lost. His tongue reached out to hers, coaxing, thrusting, teasing. She parried his moves, savouring the thrill of his hot flesh matching her own.

'I want you so much,' he murmured against the side of her mouth as his hands slid down her back.

In response, she writhed against him, revelling in the feel of his bare skin beneath her inquisitive fingers, all thoughts of resistance lost in his first touch.

'The feeling's mutual,' she sighed as his lips found the hollow between her neck and collar-bone and nibbled gently.

'Are you sure?' His lips stilled to whisper the question, though his hands maintained their caress along her spine.

Through the haze of passion, she experienced a moment of startling clarity. Despite her doubts and fears, she needed him to make love to her. Not only needed him, she burned for him. Tonight might be the only chance she had and she was going to grab it, with both hands. It would give her something to hold on to after they parted, a precious memory she could treasure. Sliding her hands around his waist, she pulled him against her.

'I want you more than you'll ever know,' she breathed, leaning back so that they were only joined at the hip, his hands supporting her back.

'My God, you're beautiful.' The moisture between her legs increased as his gaze focused on her nipples. 'I think it's time we got you out of these clothes.'

'Shouldn't we go back to our room?' The question came out on a squeal as he peeled the spaghetti straps of her dress off her shoulders and stripped her dress to the floor, knelt before her and pressed his lips to her stomach.

'All in good time, sweetheart. I've locked the door, so we won't be disturbed here. Besides,' his tongue laved her navel, turning her legs to jelly, 'I don't think I can wait that long.'

She clung to him and closed her eyes, entwining her fingers in his hair, allowing wave after unadulterated wave of pleasure to wash over her as he placed his mouth over her most intimate place.

'Oh Matt,' she moaned.

'Feeling a bit shaky, huh?' he murmured as he eased her down on the chaise longue.

She wriggled into the plump cushions, savouring the feel of crisp cotton against her bare skin, and beckoned him with her index finger. 'Not any more. Time to return the favour.'

Matt tensed as he lowered his body into her outstretched arms, desperately trying to stay in control. The moisture on his skin had evaporated with the heat generated between their bodies, only to be replaced with a light film of sweat as she ran her hands down his torso. He almost lost it as her fingers slid under the elastic of his bathers and brushed him.

He groaned as her fingers closed around him and started stroking, her feather-light touch stoking his fire till he was sure he would spontaneously combust.

'Can I take these off?' Her soft question surprised him, the uncertainty in her voice in stark contrast to the experienced touch of her hand.

Their gazes locked, the vulnerability in her green depths tugging at his heart. He leaned forward and clasped her head, caressing her ears with his thumbs. 'Go for it.'

His heart lifted in response to her tremulous smile. 'Though I won't be responsible for my actions after that…'

'I'm willing to take the risk,' she responded, her stare never leaving his for an instant.

CHAPTER TEN

So much for pretending to be Matt's girlfriend over the weekend. After their lovemaking session by the pool Kara had slipped into the role with renewed gusto, all previous doubts banished. They had made love the whole night once back in their room, exploring each other's bodies till dawn. Several people had remarked on her glow the next day, particularly Jeff. Funny how he'd been the person she'd been most concerned about fooling, thinking he would discover that she was a fake.

Instead, no one needed convincing because she'd fallen into her role only too well. It had been surprisingly easy to ignore her niggling fears when Matt treated her like his queen, constantly touching her as if to reassure himself that she was really there. They had gone horse riding that afternoon, breaking away from the main group to find a sheltered spot among the eucalyptus. There, on the shady banks of the river, they had kissed like a couple of teenagers, rarely coming up for air. If it hadn't been for the untimely approach of a curious wallaby, they would have taken their roll in the grass just one step further.

Dinner had been a breeze, though his wandering

hand under the tablecloth proved a tad distracting when trying to maintain a civilised conversation with other table occupants. His father had smiled indulgently whenever she'd caught his stare across the table and she'd repressed a hint of guilt at what she was doing.

For there could be no doubt that the situation was still wrong. Matt was using her to dupe his father and she was going along with it, all in the name of some stupid deal. And not just for Sally, if she was completely honest with herself. She loved being his girlfriend and their perfect physical compatibility merely emphasised the fact. Simply, she loved him. And there wasn't a damn thing she could do about it.

'Doing some serious thinking, huh?'

She glanced across at his profile, her pulse accelerating. 'I was just thinking about last night.'

'Me too.' He swerved the car to miss an ambling wombat on the side of the road. 'See? It's not good for my health. Too distracting.'

She laughed, reaching over and placing a hand on his thigh. 'Is that so? I read somewhere that physical exertion of the indoor variety is extremely beneficial for one's health, particularly the heart.'

He laid a hand over hers and said cheekily, 'And other parts of the anatomy.'

She snatched her hand away and slapped his. 'Concentrate on the road.'

'Easy for you to say. I have to contend with the most beautiful woman in the world sitting next to me. How's a man supposed to concentrate on anything, let alone the road?'

A thrill of delight raced through her at his compliment. 'I'm sure you'll manage. After all, you seemed pretty confident in doing several things at once last night.'

He growled suggestively in response and they passed the next half-hour in companionable silence, lost in their own thoughts. Too soon, they arrived at her town house. She'd dreaded this moment, wondering if the weekend had been a figment of her imagination and their new-found relationship would vanish on their return to Sydney. So much for playing it cool. The weekend had merely entrenched her love for him and she'd fallen hook, line and sinker. She just hoped he wouldn't take one look at her now and throw her back into the pond.

'Do you have the keys?' he enquired, dropping her bag on the doorstep.

She nodded, fumbling in her handbag. 'Just a sec.' She couldn't read the expression in his eyes. The blue of his shirt enhanced their fathomless depths, increasing her nervousness.

'Want me to help?' He reached across and plucked

her keys from the side-pocket, a hint of a smile tugging at the corners of his mouth. He opened the door in a second and deposited her bag inside. 'I have to go. Business at the office.'

Her heart plummeted. She'd hoped he would come in and they could discuss what had happened. Instead, he was only too eager to escape her company, by going to the office on a Sunday? Lame, even by his standards.

'Thanks for the weekend. I had a good time.' She almost cringed at the predictable words, unable to meet his eyes.

He tilted her chin up and dropped a light kiss on her lips. 'I'll call you, OK?'

She managed a feeble smile as he whirled around and walked down the path. He didn't look back. Retrieving the keys and closing the door with a sigh, she heard the car roar away. It was only as she placed the keys on the entrance table did she remember the other key. In the midst of their overwhelming passion, she'd forgotten about the key he'd given her.

So much for unlocking his secrets. He hadn't needed to challenge her with that tempting key. She'd taken one look at his wet body and lost her mind. The trouble was, her heart had followed suit and she had no idea how to retrieve either.

* * *

The doorbell roused her. Glancing around, Kara was surprised to see twilight had descended; she must have fallen asleep on the couch.

'Who is it?' She rubbed her gritty eyes, wishing whoever it was would go away. Sunday nights were her 'chill-out' time in preparation for the dreaded Monday mornings.

'Open up, chickadee.'

Sal launched her large body at Kara the moment she opened the door and enveloped her in a bear hug. 'How are you, darling? How was the weekend? How's that gorgeous boyfriend of yours?'

She held up her hands in surrender. 'One at a time, Sal.'

Sally eyed her critically. 'What's up with you? I thought you'd be over the moon after spending the weekend with that dishy hunk of yours.'

'He's not mine,' she muttered, wishing the words weren't true.

'Is that right? Well, how do you explain that look you've got? The one that says you haven't slept a wink in the last few nights, huh?' Sal folded her arms over her ample bosom and grinned.

Kara blushed, heat creeping into her cheeks. 'I don't know what you're talking about. I was just having a snooze. That's why I look tired.' She turned away and filled the kettle, knowing her face would give away her secrets.

The older woman came up behind and hugged her.

'I'm not prying, darling. I'm just so happy that you and Matt have found each other again.'

'Mmm...' Sal's hug almost undid her completely. She longed to turn around, bury herself in Sal's arms and confide the whole sordid mess: the deal, the money, her feelings for Matt. Pulling herself together, she broke the embrace and buried her head in the refrigerator in search of the milk.

'I've got some news for you. Big news.' Sal's voice brimmed with excitement.

As Kara turned, Sal started punching the air. 'I won! Can you believe it? I actually won!'

Realisation and all its implications hit like a freight train. Matchmaker had won the DATY.

'That's fantastic. Congratulations, Sal. I knew you could do it.' Kara hugged Sal, amazed that the first seed of doubt sprouted in the midst of her happiness. If the DATY was Sal's, she had no reason to pose as Matt's girlfriend any more. Not on her part, anyway.

'Thanks, darling. If it weren't for you, none of this would've happened. The judges said that matching my thousandth couple swayed their decision. Speaking of which, I'll need you and Matt to do some publicity stuff.'

Dread stole into her heart. 'What sort of stuff?' If she was going to come clean with Matt, how could she expect him to take part in publicity?

Sally shrugged. 'I'm not sure yet, though the judges will let me know. See, everything turned out for the best. I won the award, the agency is saved with the prize money and you got your man. Matchmaker to the rescue again.' She licked her finger and chalked one up in the air.

You got your man.

Sal's words echoed through her mind. If only they were true. Instead, she now had to call the whole deal off and he would find some other woman to take her place, probably in the blink of an eye. Sure, he would be annoyed that the charade would start all over again but he would eventually get the partnership he longed for. She was the one who had come off second best. In helping to save Sal's business, she'd lost her heart. Again. To the same man. How on earth would she recover from that? There was only one thing to do and she wasn't looking forward to it. Not one little bit.

Thankfully, Sal didn't stay long, giving Kara a chance to do some serious thinking before she approached Matt with the news that their deal was off. Heck, she would miss him. More than that, how would she cope with seeing him with another woman, now that she'd completely lost her mind and fallen in love with him all over again?

She'd known that getting physical with him would solidify her feelings yet she'd thrown caution to the wind and done it anyway. So much for erecting barriers. So much for pushing him away. The minute Matt had re-entered her life, she should have done the only sane thing possible…move to Perth!

Instead, she'd followed her heart, which was about to get its comeuppance. For there was no doubting that she would come off second best when this deal ended: no more dinners, no more phone calls, no more shared intimacy where Matt's skill and attention made her body sing.

Suddenly, a smidgeon of an idea insinuated its way into her thoughts. If she had to tell him the truth, why not take one last chance at grabbing happiness? If she could make him want her more than anything and let him have a final taste of what he would be missing out on if he gave her up, maybe, just maybe, they could have their fairy-tale ending after all?

She bit back a grin as the idea solidified, modified and finally took flight. Yeah, she could pull this off and she knew just what she needed to put her plan into action.

Matt signed the last contract, added it to the pile and leaned back in his chair. It had been a gruelling fortnight, with several key negotiations drawing to a close almost simultaneously. God, he was tired but invigorated at the same time, the thrill of success just as sweet now as it was when he'd done his first deal.

He loved his work and he was going to love being
a partner in the firm even more.

Not as much as you could love Kara.

Matt just had to see her. She'd sounded cool on
the phone the few times they had spoken lately. What
had happened to the fiery temptress who had whispered and moaned beneath him?

A knock on the door interrupted his thoughts.

'Go away, Saunders. I'm not in the mood.' He'd
been anticipating a visit from his friend, hell-bent on
giving him the usual third degree about Kara.

'Oh? Are you in the mood for anything else?'

He sat bolt upright, stunned as the woman he'd
just been fantasising about materialised before his
eyes. What was more, her voice matched the one in
his head, all breathy and seductive. And the get-up!
The long trench coat, belted at the waist, hid God
only knew what.

'What are you doing here?' he managed to croak,
clearing his throat, which sounded like a pond of
frogs in chorus.

In reply, she shut and bolted the door. As she
turned back, he caught a tantalising glimpse of lace-
topped stocking. Lord, she wasn't wearing a skirt.
His heart stopped beating for a second at the thought
she wasn't wearing anything at all, then proceeded
to gallop away at a million beats a minute.

'You've been avoiding me.' She waggled her finger at him as she perched on the edge of his desk. 'So I decided to remedy the situation.'

He shifted in his seat, unable to tear his gaze away from her endless legs, criss-crossed just centimetres away from his face. He needed to get up, to get away before he reached towards her. However, the tempting vision sitting in front of him had inflamed his libido further and there was no way he could get up and let her see him like this: wanting, eager, burning for her.

Struggling to keep his cool, he tore his gaze away from her legs. Unfortunately, staring into her eyes wasn't much better. Their luminous glow matched the lawyer's lamp on his desk, a deep, shadowed green, casting a muted light over everything in its path.

'Are you here to talk?' He swallowed, trying to dismiss the ardent gleam in her eyes as a figment of his wishful imagination.

'Sort of.'

She slid off the desk and stood in front of him. His heart pounded as she fiddled with the coat's belt and its giant buttons. Surely she wasn't going to take it off, right here in his office? His fingers clenched, gripping the chair arms like a drowning man grabbing hold of a lifebuoy. For he was drowning, drowning in a wave of sizzling lust like he'd never experienced before.

'What does that mean?'

'I think it's time we sorted out a few things, don't you?'

Her hands had stilled but his imagination didn't, and in an instant he'd jumped to his feet and pinned her against the desk, holding her hands behind her back.

'You call this talking?' Kara murmured, pressing her body to his, tilting her head back to welcome his kiss.

Matt's lips devoured her, nibbling and tasting with the abandon of a starving man. It was no ordinary kiss and there was nothing sweet about it. Kara opened her mouth to him, drawing him to her.

'I like the language you speak.' His mouth broke contact as he traced a feather-light trail down her cheek.

So much for being the one in control. She'd hoped to drive Matt wild with need yet all she'd done was inflame her own. Not that she had much say in it. At the moment, her body was doing all the talking.

'I've missed you,' she said, clinging to him.

'Likewise.' He pulled away and looked down. She squirmed under his scrutiny, suddenly vulnerable. 'That's some get-up you're almost wearing.'

'What, this old thing? I use it all the time, to tempt pigheaded men to see what they're missing out on.'

'You'd better not.' He crushed her to him, kissing her emphatically to prove the point.

'Uh, Matt?' Her hands trailed down his back, before grabbing his butt.

'Mmm?' He clenched his muscles, laughing at the surprised look on her face.

'Your place or mine?' The soft, upward curl of his smile focused her attention on his lips, and for a moment she wondered if she had the courage to go through with the rest of her plan.

'That's what I like. A forward woman.' He grabbed his keys and shrugged into his jacket. 'You decide.'

'Mine,' she said quickly, before she lost her nerve totally. 'As for being forward, you ain't seen nothing yet…'

CHAPTER ELEVEN

KARA couldn't go through with it. She'd planned on telling Matt the truth once they had breakfast but hadn't got round to it. In fact, she hadn't had a chance, as breakfast had turned into a repeat of the night before. They had laughed afterwards while cradling steaming cups of freshly brewed coffee, making jokes about the kettle not being the only thing letting off steam.

It wasn't just the kitchen. His memory was everywhere now, in every nook and cranny of her house. She'd wanted it that way, giving her some small part of him to cherish when she ended it. Sure, she'd succeeded with most of her plan. She just hadn't been able to see it to completion. The part about calling it quits had slipped her mind about the time the trench coat came off at her front door. And the rest of the night and the morning had been less than conducive to ending their relationship.

She couldn't believe she'd pulled off that performance in his office last night. It had been part of her master plan to make love one last time, to drive him mad with wanting her, to make him remember her before calling the deal off. For the longer she continued the charade as his girlfriend, the longer it would take her heart to mend. If ever.

Now that her feelings of guilt about Sal had been resolved, she'd thrown herself into the role of his girlfriend with the selfish wish to please herself. It wasn't as if she was doing anything terribly wrong. She had no intention of taking the money at the end of the deal and she wasn't deceiving anybody.

Except herself.

If she was completely honest, she still harboured the fantasy that he'd fall in love with her and they would live happily ever after, just as the fairy tale promised. However, she wasn't Cinderella and she had the distinct impression that her Prince Charming was about to ride off into the sunset without her.

The doorbell rang as she finished applying a slick of lipstick. Another bonus: being a stickler for punctuality, Matt was always on time. She opened the door with a flourish.

'Hi there.' She kept her greeting simple, as she could hardly speak when confronted by the mouth-watering sight of Matt Byrne in a tux.

'Hi there yourself.' He let out a long, low wolf-whistle, grabbed her hands and twirled her around. 'You look fantastic.' Pulling her flush against him, he backed her inside and slammed the door with a kick of his foot.

'Glad you approve,' she murmured, wrapping her arms around him, enjoying the feel of his freshly shaved cheek against her own and the intoxicating scent of his signature aftershave.

'Oh, I do…very much.' He leaned his hips into her. 'I think you can tell just how much.'

His hardness drove all thought of the evening ahead from her mind as she entwined a leg around his, sliding it up and down. 'Just how important is this cocktail party?' Her voice sounded as if it came from a distant planet as her heartbeat reverberated in her ears.

Backing her up against the entry-hall mirror, he kissed her thoroughly before pulling away. 'I'm sorry, sweetheart. I'd like nothing better than to continue this but my dad's making a big announcement tonight. I need to be there. If it's what I think it is…' He trailed off, not needing to say the words.

She disengaged herself from his arms and stepped away, eager to put some distance between them so she could think straight. 'So, tonight's the night?'

'I'm not sure, but what else could it be? There's been a spot vacant for a partner for the last few months and Dad's been sizing me up.' He stalked around the lounge, looking increasingly nervous. 'I've done everything he suggested…' Once-again, he didn't finish the sentence. He didn't have to. They both knew he was talking about the deal, and if tonight's announcement went according to expectations he wouldn't need to continue their charade any longer.

'You sure have.' She tried to keep her tone light-hearted and failed miserably.

'I'm sorry, Kara. For everything.' Thankfully, he didn't come near her.

'Don't apologise. We both knew the score at the start. A deal's a deal, remember?' She'd mastered a flippant tone where he was concerned. It was the only way to hide the hurt.

He had the grace to look sheepish. 'Yeah, but I didn't plan on taking it all the way.' He paused and looked away. 'Uh…I mean about us…you know…'

'Having sex, you mean? God, Matt, for a lawyer you can be pretty hopeless with words sometimes.'

That captured his attention. His gaze swivelled towards her. 'Don't you think it complicates things?'

She shrugged and turned away. 'Why should it? You make partner, I make a lot of money. Done deal.' She rifled through her evening bag, in desperate need of a tissue. A tear threatened to seep out of the corner of her eye and she needed to blot it away, fast. Hopefully, the mention of the money might divert his attention away from their relationship and onto safer ground. It did.

'Yeah, whatever you say. By the way, why do you need thirty grand anyway?' He avoided touching her as he swung the door shut and followed her to the car.

'It's not important now, so let's drop it.' She struggled to maintain composure, knowing that this evening would be the longest of her entire life.

Tension radiated from him like heat from a furnace and she was happy when they sped away from the kerb and he hit 'play' on the latest CD to avoid further conversation.

She wondered why he was so angry. She'd merely stated the facts: they had a deal, which had been his idea, they had made love, but it would all end when he made partner. As far as she could see, everything had worked out in his favour. *He* wasn't the one who had been foolish enough to fall in love along the way. If anyone should be upset, it was she. As long as she lived, she'd never figure men out.

'We're here.' Short, sharp, to the point. No use mincing words when you were about to get everything you'd dreamed about. Lucky him.

She schooled her features into a polite mask as he opened the car door for her. 'Good luck tonight.' Her voice didn't waver, despite her heart breaking at the thought of losing him.

'Thanks. Let's hope we both get our dues.' He stared at her a fraction too long before guiding her to the elevator and up to the penthouse where his father now lived.

As the lift whizzed up to the top floor, she couldn't help but remember riding the same elevator up to the twenty-fifth floor, where his office was located. She'd been just as nervous then as she was now but for a different reason. The way Matt was standing on the other side of the elevator with his hands thrust into his pockets, there wasn't a hope in hell of them ever touching again, let alone making love.

His low voice startled her. 'Uh, once this deal is over, let's...' The elevator door opened and Jeff, resplendent in formal attire, beamed at them.

'Great to see you, son. And you're looking as beautiful as ever, Kara. What did this guy here do to deserve someone like you?' He punched Matt playfully on the arm.

Try buying me to convince you to give him a partnership.

The way Matt glared at her, she had a horrifying feeling that she'd spoken out loud. Instead, he ground out, 'Just lucky, I guess, Dad. So what's going on?'

'All in good time, son, all in good time. Come in and make yourselves at home.' Jeff winked at them before striding away.

'Fat chance of that happening,' Matt muttered as Lorna strutted across the room towards them.

'Well, well, if it isn't my darling stepson. Come and give your mama a kiss.' The simpering voice didn't match the coldness flashing in her blue eyes.

Kara almost recoiled as the cool blonde draped herself over Matt and kissed him on the lips, lingering a tad too long to be familial. She'd only met her briefly at a dinner party several months ago, the older woman barely giving her a second look. Surprisingly, she turned to her now.

'Oh, and if it isn't sweet little Lara. Jeff sings your praises all the time.' She extended a bejewelled hand, as if expecting her to bow over it.

'It's Kara, actually. How are you?' Determined to be polite, she yearned to smack the other woman's hand away as it rested possessively on Matt's arm.

'Fine, dear. Though I'm looking forward to the fun and games. Big announcement tonight. Huge. Hope you like it.' She blew Matt a kiss before sashaying away, a tall, thin figure in a stunning dress that must have cost as much as Kara earned in a month.

'God, I hate that woman.' Matt spat the words out, glaring daggers at the retreating back.

'Why wasn't she at the King River weekend?' Not particularly interested in the answer, Kara was just happy to be talking with Matt again.

'Probably off with her latest gigolo. Who knows? Who cares? I just wish Dad would wake up to her. If it's one thing I can't stand, it's a woman deceiving her man.'

That captured her attention. What would he think if she told him the truth right now, that she hadn't been interested in the money all along, that she'd played along with his stupid deal for Sal's sake, and later for her own? Not willing to go there for the moment, she deflected some of the heat back on to him.

'What about a man deceiving his father? Is that OK?' The words hung in the silence between them and for a split-second she wished she could take them back. However, it was the truth and she was tired of playing games.

His eyes narrowed, fury evident in the set of his shoulders and tense neck muscles. 'I told you once before not to question me about this. I have my reasons.' He spun on his heel and strode away.

Yeah, selfish reasons. Obtaining a partnership being the main one. She picked up a champagne flute from a passing waiter and downed it in three short gulps, hoping it would dissolve the lump of emotion stuck in her throat.

Yeah, she remembered when he'd told her not to question him and it seemed like a lifetime ago rather than a few short months. Watching him deep in conversation with his father across the room, she vowed to tell him the truth. The whole truth. At that moment, Jeff Byrne cleared his throat.

'Ladies and gentlemen, can I have your attention?' Voices petered out as all eyes turned to him.

'As you all know, Byrne and Associates have had

a vacancy for a partner over the last few months, and tonight I'm happy to announce that the position has now been filled.'

An excited twittering filled the room.

'The man in question has brought many new clients to the firm and has shown me that he has what it takes to make it in this business.'

She glanced at Matt, who had moved away and was standing next to the floor-to-ceiling window that overlooked the stunning harbour bridge, lit like a giant, sparkling coat-hanger. She sensed rather than saw his excitement as he sipped from a whisky tumbler, his lips compressed into a thin line.

'So, without further ado, I'd like to present the new partner. Please welcome Steve Rockwell to the firm.'

Scattered applause and gasps of surprise filled the room. She watched in horror as her ex sauntered out of the kitchen and walked up to shake Jeff's hand, flashing that all-too-familiar crocodile smile. As if in slow motion, she saw Matt almost stagger backwards and lean against the window, his mouth gaping.

Willing her legs to move, she walked towards him as the first strains of *For He's a Jolly Good Fellow* filtered through the room. Grabbing the glass from Matt's hand and placing it on a nearby table, she stood on tiptoe and whispered in his ear, 'Let's get out of here.'

He looked down at her as if seeing her for the first time. At least he'd finally closed his jaw.

'Come on.' She tugged on his arm. 'Whatever you're thinking of doing, it's not worth it.'

The expression in his eyes tore at her soul, a mixture of hurt, anger and gut-wrenching betrayal. 'Easy for you to say. You're not the one whose father just kicked you in the teeth without having the decency to tell you first.'

She kept her voice deliberately low, soothing. 'I know it's hard but just think for a second. You have to face these people at work tomorrow and no matter how much you want to slug Steve, forget it. How you handle yourself now will make a lasting impression, particularly on your father.'

He took several breaths, inhaling and exhaling as his clenched facial muscles slowly relaxed. 'Who gives a damn what he thinks?'

'You do,' she murmured. 'Otherwise you wouldn't have come up with such an elaborate plan to secure a partnership. Handling me for six months is no picnic, you know.'

He looked at her with a glimmer of a smile. 'Oh, I don't know about that. *Handling* you has been a lot more fun than expected.'

Her heart leaped as a flicker of warmth returned to his eyes. She squeezed his hand, returning his smile. 'Why don't you head over there, congratulate

Steve and show your dad that Matthew Byrne is definitely partner material next time round?'

'Don't push it,' he growled. 'I'd rather shake hands with a crocodile than Rockwell.'

The imagery did it. She cracked up, laughing till she almost cried.

'What's so funny?'

Wiping her eyes, she let him in on the secret. 'I was thinking along similar lines myself, that's all. Don't you think he grins like a croc?'

He glanced in Steve's direction. 'Sure does. You're the one who went out with him for years though. Does he have scaly skin to match?'

She raised her eyebrows.

'On second thoughts, don't answer that.'

She marvelled at the way his anger had diffused. He hadn't just lost a dream, he'd lost it to a man he didn't like. She felt him stiffen and looked up. Steve was walking towards them.

Matt held out his hand. 'Congratulations, Rockwell.'

'No hard feelings, eh, Byrne?'

The men shook on it, yet she had the distinct impression the games were only just beginning.

'Well done, Steve.' If Matt could do it, so could she.

'Thanks, honey.' Steve puffed up, looking a million dollars in his tuxedo and knowing it. 'We'll have to get together some time.' Before she could move, he dropped a quick peck on her cheek and strode away.

'Over my dead body,' she heard Matt mutter. 'He still has a thing for you.'

'Do you think?' She batted her eyelashes, keen to make him laugh again.

He rolled his eyes. 'Women! Let me have a quick word with Dad and I'll meet you by the elevator, OK?'

She watched with pride as he walked up to a group of men including his father, and joined in their conversation. It took a big man to do what he'd just done and she loved him all the more for it. Seeing Lorna join the group, she quickly vowed to tell him the truth. He hated deception so she would lay it on the line. What was the worst that could happen? *He'll never speak to you again. You'll lose him. Again.*

Fighting back the tears, she turned away. Tomorrow. She would do it then. Surely it wouldn't be selfish to have just one more night?

Kara took a few deep, steadying breaths and knocked on the door.

'Come in.'

She pushed open the door to Matt's office and walked in.

'Hey, just the lady I was thinking about.' He stood

up and walked around the desk, enveloping her in a hug. 'God, you smell good,' he whispered against her hair.

She pulled away, trying to put some distance between them. Otherwise, she wouldn't be able to go through with this. 'Do you have a minute?'

'I've always got time for you. Especially in this office…' He patted the desk, reviving memories of their passionate encounter.

Rather than the heat dissipating, her cheeks inflamed further as she cleared her throat. 'We need to talk.'

The smile left his face. 'Oh-oh. When a woman says ''we need to talk'', it usually means ''I'm doing the talking and you sure as hell better listen, mister''. Correct?'

She shook her head. 'No, though it wouldn't do you any harm if you did listen for a change.'

His eyebrows shot up. 'Fine. Take a seat and let me have it. I'm all ears.'

Go on. Tell him. You can do it.

As she opened her mouth to speak, his phone rang.

'Excuse me.' He reached for the phone, speaking in hushed tones, annoyance evident in his face.

She let out a whoosh of breath, unaware she'd been holding it. This was going to be harder than she'd thought. She'd chosen his office to tell him the truth for a specific reason. They would need to keep their voices lowered and there was little chance that he could distract her with his physical talents. At least not during office hours anyway.

It was cowardly but she had no other option. If she'd told him anywhere else and he'd tried to change her mind about continuing the deal, she doubted whether she'd be able to resist him. After all, he could be very persuasive when he tried. And the way they had been spending every spare minute in bed together, she should know.

He slammed the phone down, making her jump. 'Sorry. I really need to see someone for a minute. Do you mind waiting?'

'No, go ahead. I'll grab a coffee.'

'Thanks. This shouldn't take longer than ten minutes. Come straight in when you get back.' He paused for a moment, rifling through a stack of papers on his desk, looking increasingly distracted.

As she opened the door, almost relieved to get a reprieve from telling him the truth, he spoke.

'I'm glad you dropped by today. I agree that it's time we talked.'

She turned and caught him staring at her with such an intense look on his face that it took her breath away. She nodded and smiled, suddenly anxious to leave the stifling atmosphere of his office.

What was she thinking? No matter where or when she told him the truth, it wasn't going to be easy.

Hoping that an injection of strong caffeine might help calm her nerves, she ignored the doubts whirling through her mind and managed to scan the latest trashy magazine while getting her coffee fix. At least other people had lives as complicated as hers, even if half of the stories were invented by the paparazzi. Glancing at her watch, she was surprised to see that ten minutes had lapsed. Time to face the music.

However, as she knocked lightly on Matt's door and opened it, she wished she'd had something stronger than coffee to fortify her. He was deep in conversation with Steve and it was obvious what they were discussing as the words 'thirty thousand dollars' and 'she earned it' reached her ears.

She made a strangled sound and Matt leaped up, his stricken look freezing her heart. 'I can explain. The truth is—'

'The truth?' Kara strode into the room and stopped two paces short of his desk. 'You wouldn't know what that was if it leaped up and bit you on the butt! Let me tell you a few truths...' Her voice had risen in fury and she couldn't stop it.

'Stop right there.' He spoke quietly and she followed his glance, which was fixed on his father, who had just entered the office.

'No.' She folded her arms, wishing she could contain the pain in her heart, the offending organ threatening to burst out of her chest if it kept up its furious pounding. She was past the point of caring, all the uncertainty, the deception and the hurt of the last few months building up to this confrontation.

'You want the truth, Matt? The truth, the whole truth and nothing but the truth? Well, here goes.'

CHAPTER TWELVE

'DON'T do this, Kara.' Matt kept his voice devoid of all emotion though fear threatened to reduce him to a stuttering mess. The irrational fear of having this confrontation in front of his father and the mind-numbing fear of losing the woman who meant everything to him.

'And don't tell me what to do,' she spat out, her angry glare fixed on him.

'It's not what it looks like. Steve and I were discussing...' He broke off as he caught a glimpse of tears in Kara's eyes. Even at such an inopportune time, he noticed how beautiful she looked: arms crossed, breasts heaving, the tears lending a shimmer to her green eyes. His heart constricted as he recognised just how much she meant to him. At a crazy time like this, it hit him that he might actually love her. *Great.*

Kara glared at Steve, who hadn't said a word since she had come in.

'You two best buddies now? Swapping stories?' Kara spoke with deadly precision, not a quiver in her voice. It chilled him to the bone.

Matt shook his head. 'Don't be ridiculous. I—'

'Ridiculous? Well, that's funny coming from you. Couldn't be more ridiculous than paying someone to pose as your girlfriend just to obtain a partnership in Daddy's firm.'

There was pin-drop silence. He stared at Kara in horror, hearing but not quite believing she'd just said that. His gaze shifted beyond her to his father, who stood in the doorway and hadn't said a word up to this point. Jeff's face turned puce as he took a step into the room and took control.

'Steve, please leave. My son and I need to sort out some issues.'

As if it were happening in slow motion, Matt watched Steve shake his head and leave the room. Kara looked set to follow.

'I want you to stay, Kara.' Though his father spoke softly, Matt knew that tone. It wasn't a request, it was a command. Surprisingly Kara did too, for she stopped in mid-stride.

'There's nothing left for me to say,' she said, her gaze firmly focused on his father. 'This is between you and him.' She pointed towards Matt with a jerk of her head, not even glancing in his direction.

'I know, but you're involved too. Please stay.' His dad walked towards her and enveloped her in a hug. It was exactly what Matt wanted to do at that moment, but couldn't. The way she'd looked at him earlier, he seriously doubted he would ever have that opportunity again.

What had he done?

His father's next words merely served to reinforce the fact that he hadn't just lost Kara, he'd lost any hope of gaining his father's respect also.

'I can't believe a son of mine would try to buy his way into a promotion, let alone use a lovely woman to get there.' His dad shook his head, before fixing Matt with a steely stare. 'What the hell are you playing at?'

Matt couldn't speak for a moment as Kara finally turned to face him again. The sight of tears trickling down her cheeks hit him like a fist to his gut: swift, sharp, agonising. It took his breath away.

He sat there for a moment, riveted by two pairs of eyes, one a murderous blue so like his own in colour, and the other a luminous green that clearly showed hurt in its depths. There was only one way out of this. As she'd said, it was time for the truth. The whole truth.

He stood up and approached his father. 'I know how this looks but I have my reasons.'

His father held up his hands. 'Stop right there. What you've done is inexcusable, reasons or not. My God, what were you thinking? Paying Kara to be your girlfriend, all for the damn partnership?'

Matt shook his head. 'Not just for that,' he murmured.

'What?' his father barked.

It was now or never. Matt had to lay everything on the line if he was to salvage anything out of this mess.

'It wasn't just about being made partner, Dad. It's about you and me, about you recognising me as your son, about you approving of me.' He paused for only a second, afraid that if he didn't reveal his feelings now, he never would. 'All I've ever wanted was for you to approve of me, to recognise my achievements…' He trailed off, the look of horror on his father's face more than a match for the look of shock on Kara's, both gut-wrenching.

'But I do approve of you, son. I've always been proud of you.'

'No, Dad. You occasionally talk to me about business but when was the last time you really took notice of me, other than to berate me about my private life?'

His father was silent, staring at him as if he were an alien life form.

Matt continued, 'Ever since Mum left, I've felt like an outsider, as if I was a burden to you. Your wives were more important than me. You want to know why being made partner was so damn important to me? Because I was fool enough to think it might bring us closer together. Stupid, huh?' He sank into the nearest chair and dropped his head in his hands, totally drained.

'Son?' His father laid a hand on his slumped shoulder.

'Just leave it, Dad. I need to talk to Kara now. Alone.'

The grip on his shoulder tightened. 'I'm sorry for making you feel second best, Matthew. That was never my intention. I only wanted what's best for you and that meant building up my business to provide you with a stable future. As for your mother, there isn't a day that goes by that I don't berate myself for chasing away the best thing that ever happened to me…' The words choked off and Matt finally looked up.

His father's eyes glistened. For the first time in his life, he saw his father moved to tears and it shocked him more than anything else could have.

'Dad, I—'

'No, let me finish. I admit I haven't been the best father in the world, but throwing myself into the business was the only way I knew how to cope. Spending time with you was out of the question, as you're so much like her. Every time you looked up at me I saw her eyes, her pain. It would break my heart all over again.'

He ran his hands through his peppery hair. 'Poor

excuse, I know, but it's how I felt. By the time you were grown up, it was too late. The divide was there between us and I never had the guts to broach it. Can you forgive me?'

Matt stood up and opened his arms. For the first time since he was six years old, his father hugged him. Not just a pat on the back or a ruffling of his hair but a real bear hug. A weight lifted from his shoulders as he swallowed, trying to dislodge the lump of emotion stuck in his throat.

'There's nothing to forgive, Dad. We're both lousy communicators, that's all.' His voice sounded shaky, even to his own ears. He'd almost fooled himself that everything was all right, till he looked over his father's shoulder and saw Kara staring at him. Suddenly the weight descended again, and this time it was ten times heavier.

His father must have sensed the tightening of his shoulders, for he pulled back with a speculative gleam in his eyes. 'We can talk later. Right now there's a young lady here who deserves your apology more than me.'

He watched his dad give Kara a peck on the cheek. 'Don't let him off too easy. He deserves everything he gets.'

With a fond smile at them both, he left the office.

Kara stared at Matt in stunned amazement. She couldn't believe that he hadn't thought enough of

their friendship to tell her all that stuff about his father. So much for hoping he might fall in love with
her and reciprocate her feelings. Over all the dates,
the dinners and, lately, the mornings spent cuddled
together in bed, he hadn't whispered one word of the
truth to her. It hurt more than anything he could have
said to her.

All she'd been to him was a means to an end. So
the deal included sex? No worries for Matt. He'd
taken what was on offer, no regrets, no recrimina-
tions. And to think she'd come here today to tell him
the truth!

'Why don't we sit down and talk?' His low voice
broke into her thoughts.

She stared at him, amazed he could look so calm.

'I don't think so. There's not much left to say, is
there? You've made peace with your father, what
more is there? The deal's over.'

His expression changed from one of abject sadness
to cold anger in a second. 'So, that's what you came
here to talk about today? The dating deal. It always
came back to the money for you, didn't it?'

Fighting back the tears yet again, she managed to
keep her voice steady. 'Whatever. I don't care any
more.'

'Well, I care,' he spat out, sitting at his desk and
yanking open the top drawer.

He scrawled something in a booklet and tore it out. With dawning horror, she realised what it was.

'Here, take it. You *earned* it.' He thrust the cheque into her hands, strode towards the door and opened it for her.

An icy fist reached around her heart and squeezed, threatening to shatter it into a million aching pieces. She looked up at him but he refused to make eye contact. As she stared at the cheque in her hand the figures swam before her eyes. He actually believed she'd come this far for thirty thousand dollars? She'd revealed more of herself to this man than to anyone else and he didn't have a clue.

She willed her legs to move, taking one robotic step after another towards the door.

'Here. This belongs to you.'

She stood in front of him and ripped the cheque into pieces, letting them drop when he continued to ignore her. They slowly drifted to the floor and lay in a scattered mess.

Just like your dreams, she thought as she brushed past him for the final time.

Matt slammed the door after Kara had left, hard enough to shake the walls. Thank God he didn't have glass partitioning like some of the other lawyers—it would have smashed in a second. Not to mention the fact it would have given them a bird's-eye view of the fiasco that had just taken place in here.

He stared at the torn remnants of the cheque at his feet. For some reason, they frightened him. He thought he'd had her all figured out. She'd come here today to push him to conclude the deal after he hadn't made partner last night. She obviously thought that she'd earned her money, despite the fact he hadn't got what he wanted.

If she only knew that the longer their charade had gone on, the less important the partnership became. *She*'d been the reason he'd continued their stupid deal and his irrational, all-consuming feelings for her had wiped away any semblance of common sense he once possessed. So much for being the cool lawyer, the consummate performer. He'd acted like a consummate jackass!

Yes, she'd certainly played him for a fool. He'd started to believe that she might actually feel something for him, regardless of the bloody deal. But no. She'd turned up today to call the shots.

But if the money was the only thing she wanted, why tear up the cheque?

It didn't make sense. The more he thought about it, the more confused he became. He should be ecstatic now. He'd finally patched things up with his dad, he didn't have to pretend with Kara any more...

That was it. Instead of feeling ten feet tall, he felt

like a miner trapped beneath ten feet of rubble. He didn't have to pretend with her any more, which meant he could tell her the truth. He loved her, had probably never stopped loving her all these years. She was the only woman who had ever made him feel whole, which was why he felt as if his soul had been torn in half.

She'd walked away. Correction, he'd pushed her away. Without telling her the truth. He'd made a mess of it again, just as he had on her eighteenth birthday. Would he ever learn?

Propelled into action, he raced towards the lift. If he was lucky, she'd still be in the foyer. Tapping his foot impatiently as the lift sped towards the ground floor, he tried mentally rehearsing what he would say and came up strangely lacking. For once, his quick mind had deserted him. He would have to wing it and hope to God that his negotiation skills kicked in at the right time.

As the lift doors opened, he had a vague idea of what he'd say. However, his declaration of love stuck in his throat when he saw Kara in the arms of Steve Rockwell.

So, he'd been right after all. She'd made her choice and it wasn't him. He stumbled back into the lift, punching the button for the twenty-fifth floor several times before hitting the target and berating himself for being a gullible fool.

*   *   *

Kara's feet dragged as she found her way to a nearby café and ordered her second coffee in less than an hour. So what if the caffeine kept her up all night? It wasn't as if she'd planned on sleeping anyway, after the disastrous end to her relationship with Matt.

Relationship? Who was she trying to kid? She'd deluded herself into believing that what she shared with Matt had been special when in fact it had been one big joke. Funnily enough, the joke was on her, though laughing was the furthest thing from her mind.

At least she understood what had just happened in Matt's office. She'd bumped into Steve in the foyer as she'd been leaving and, though he was the last person she'd expect comfort from, he'd hugged her and told her his involvement in the fiasco. He'd suspected that Matt had been up to something and confronted him with it, threatening to go to Jeff if Matt didn't come clean. Surprisingly, Matt had told him the truth about the deal, which was around the time she had come back to the office.

No matter what Steve had told her, it didn't change the facts. Matt had paid her to pose as his girlfriend and she had, she'd fallen in love and he hadn't. End of story. Even when she'd given him a final clue that it wasn't about the money on her part, he'd ignored it. After all, if he'd felt anything more than lust for her, he'd have chased after her when she'd dropped the cheque at his feet.

But he hadn't. And it was well and truly over. Time to pick up the pieces and move on. At least one good thing had come out of this mess: Sal's business had been saved and Kara had played a big part in it.

Draining the last of her coffee, she stood up, eager to get home and finally vent her feelings. Though she didn't have a cat, she had a few stress balls lying around that were going to be sore and sorry by the time she'd finished with them.

As she walked out of the café, her mobile phone rang. Staring warily at it, she checked the number on 'call display'. Matt had been ringing her on it a lot lately and he was the last person she wanted to speak to. Sadly, it took her five rings to realise that it couldn't possibly be him. He wouldn't be calling her ever again.

Thankfully, the number displayed was Sal's. With more than a hint of guilt, she hit 'divert'. She couldn't face talking to Sal right now, when she was more than likely to blab the whole sordid tale to the one person in the world who loved her unconditionally. She would ring her later, after taking time to compose herself.

She waited till the phone beeped, indicating a message had been left. Playing it back as she strolled to her car, she almost stumbled as the last part of Sal's message left a lot to be desired. In fact, her palms sweated at the thought of it.

'The DATY presentation is on tomorrow night, dear. I need you and that hunky man of yours to be there for the final publicity shots. You two look fabulous together. Great advertising for the agency. Give me a call to discuss wardrobe. Love you. Bye.'

Hah! The only thing she and Matt could advertise at the moment was an instruction manual on how to send men back to Mars and women back to Venus. And get them to stay there. Forever.

What the heck was she going to do now?

CHAPTER THIRTEEN

KARA had never been any good at hiding her emotions. It wasn't just her face that was an open book. Sal had always had the uncanny ability to hear the slightest nuance in her voice as well. And tonight had been no exception, though it probably had more to do with the fact that she'd burst into tears the minute Sal had answered the phone.

Predictably, Sal had rushed over; she'd always been there for her and Kara loved her for it. Her tears had finally dried and she was ready to talk.

'What's going on, darling? I've never seen you like this.'

The concern etched into every line of Sal's face tore at Kara's heart. She didn't want to burden her surrogate mum with the whole sordid tale, so she quickly decided to give her the edited version.

'It's a mess, Sal. My life's a shambles.'

Sal stared at her. 'You've got your own business, your own place, you've been glowing the last few months...' She trailed off and clicked her fingers. 'That's it. This is about Matt, isn't it?'

'Yeah. I think I've done something really stupid.'

Sal waved her hand, as if shooing away all her

problems. 'That's not stupid, dear, it's called having a little fun. And it's about time too!'

'I'm not talking about *that*. I think I've done something a thousand times worse.' She fiddled with the hem of her skirt, reluctant to say the words out loud.

As intuitive as ever, Sal grabbed her hand. 'You've fallen in love with him.'

It was a statement, not a question. Kara wished it wasn't true. If it had been a question, there could've been all sorts of answers and outcomes. As it was, it was a fact and there wasn't a damn thing she could do about it.

She nodded. 'See? Told you it was stupid.'

Sal squeezed her hand. 'Excuse me for being old and senile, but isn't this a good thing?'

'He doesn't love me.'

There, she'd said the words. No thunder, no lightning and she hadn't been struck down. It was only her heart that felt as if it had been electrocuted the minute she'd walked out of his office earlier, when she'd finally realised that he didn't love her.

Sal's eyebrows shot up. 'You're kidding me? The way that young man looks at you, it's positively obscene! He adores you.'

'Love isn't lust, Sal.'

'No, it's not, but Matt cares for you. Don't forget, I know people. I'm in the matchmaking business.'

Sal reminded her of a wise old sage, sitting there

in her flowing gypsy skirt and silky shawl. The image lightened her mood for the first time that day, bringing a smile to her face.

'Yeah, don't remind me. It's your fault I'm in this mess in the first place. You and your darn computer!'

Sal rolled her eyes. 'My darn computer, as you so politely put it, hasn't been wrong before.'

'Trust me. This time, it had a short circuit and a meltdown.'

They laughed. It felt wonderful for Kara, who had felt as though she would never laugh again.

'I know this throws a major spanner in the works for tomorrow night. What happens to your publicity shots?'

Sal sobered quickly. 'I need you both to be there. Wouldn't look too good if the thousandth couple broke up before the presentation. They might even take the award off me!'

For one moment, Kara could have sworn she saw a gleam of cunning in Sal's eyes, but it disappeared in a flash.

'I can't contact him, Sal. It's over.' She sighed, hating the finality of the words all over again.

'I understand, dear. Don't worry, I'll think of something.'

Sal sat back and closed her eyes, a hint of a smile tugging at the corners of her mouth.

'That's what I'm afraid of,' she muttered, wondering what Sal had in mind. The last time she'd seen that look was at the speed-dating dinner. And look where that had got her.

Sal merely grinned in response.

Matt couldn't believe he'd agreed to this. His life was slowly but surely heading down the toilet yet he'd allowed Sally to cajole him into attending her award ceremony. OK, so he'd always had a soft spot for the old lady. But why did she have to ask him at a time like this, when he was still licking his wounds?

The image of Kara in Steve Rockwell's arms was burned into his brain. Whenever he closed his eyes, there she was, tearing at his heart all over again. Dammit! Why couldn't he get her out of his head? He'd loved and left women before.

Correction, he'd liked and left them before. No woman had ever come close to capturing his love yet Kara had done it with apparently little effort. And in the process rendered him a fool. He'd never felt so stupid as he had when he'd followed her down to the foyer yesterday, only to see her in the arms of her ex.

Had she deceived him the whole time? Was she still in love with Steve and had used him? And, if so, why?

Couldn't be for the sex! Now, there was a laughable thought. A woman using a guy for sex. In his world, it had been the opposite; most of his friends would say anything to get a lovely woman into bed. Thankfully, he'd never been into casual sex, no matter what everybody thought. He'd always wooed his lady friends in the hope the relationship would develop into more. It never had. Till now.

And it was over. Wasn't it?

If he was completely honest with himself, he would admit that attending the ceremony tonight wasn't all about doing something for Sal out of the goodness of his heart. He secretly harboured the thought that Kara might show up and somehow they could work things out.

Anyone ever tell you self-delusion isn't healthy?

Reluctant to listen to his voice of reason, he'd come anyway. If anything, tonight might put some closure on the whole episode and he could move on. Somehow, the thought of moving on left a distinctly bitter taste in his mouth. However, he swallowed it, pasted a bright smile on his face and stepped from the car.

The sight of her hit him like a freight train at a million miles an hour: fast, brutal and just as damaging. He watched her glide up the front steps of the opera house, a shimmering vision in midnight shot silk that draped her lush curves and fell to her ankles. Her hair was swept up in a loose mass of curls, making her seem ten feet tall. She looked like a golden goddess, cutting a path through the crowd.

He'd never wanted her as badly as he did at that moment. He loved her and he wanted to shout it to the world. Instead, he stood there, gaping like the fool he was.

'Why don't you go after her?'

A quiet voice spoke, echoing his thoughts, and he turned to find Sally smiling at him.

He shook his head. 'I can't.'

'Can't or won't?'

'It's no use. I've blown it.' He paused, turning to stare at Kara's retreating back and wishing it wasn't true.

'Do you love her?' probed Sally, her dark eyes fixing him with a fierce stare. She reminded him of a protective Rottweiler, without the snarl and the sharp teeth.

'Yeah, I do. Not that it's done me much good.' The bitterness rose again, almost choking him.

Her expression softened and he wondered momentarily how he could have made such an unflattering comparison a few seconds ago. Kara was lucky to have someone like Sally who cared about her.

'Tell her. It's the only way.' Sally laid a hand on his back and pushed none too gently.

'What if she doesn't want to hear it?'

She raised an eyebrow, glaring at him as if he was stupid. 'What have you got to lose?'

'Everything,' he mumbled, surprised that it was true. Kara was everything to him. His lifestyle, his job and all its trappings seemed insignificant if he didn't have her.

'Go on. Don't just stand there. Do something about it.' Once again, she pushed, though this time it was more of a shove.

Suddenly, it was as if a light bulb lit up in his head. Sally was right. What did he have to lose, apart from pride?

He bent to kiss her cheek. 'Thanks, Sal. I owe you one.'

The older woman blushed. 'Now go!'

He raced after Kara, hoping it wasn't too late.

Kara entered the foyer and looked around. Sal was nowhere in sight. Great. She'd hoped to get this ordeal over and done with as soon as possible and now she would have to stand around and look interested, when all she felt like doing was running home and hiding beneath the bedcovers. If anyone approached her, she would snap.

Her nerves were stretched taut from having to pretend all day at work that nothing was wrong. She thought she'd been convincing, till one of the clients had questioned her. She'd nearly lost it then but managed to pull herself together and blame her pale list-lessness on the flu.

Having to get all dressed up in formal gear for tonight hadn't helped. She didn't feel like being glamorous, she felt downright miserable. A night at home with movies and chocolate had been the order of the day. Instead, now she had to smile and act as if she didn't have a care in the world.

For the hundredth time, she wondered what Sal would do about Matt. Perhaps she'd organised a stand-in? Imagine, two look-a-like Matt Byrnes in the world. Heck, what was she thinking? It was bad enough coping with one and she seriously doubted that any other man could pull off the *savoir-faire* that Matt possessed. It wasn't just his killer looks, his body-to-die-for or his intelligence. No, it was so much more than that…and she'd let him slip right through her fingers. He had that indefinable quality that separated the men from the boys. She wished she could bottle it, she'd make a squillion.

A passing waiter offered her a glass of champagne and she twirled the delicate crystal stem between her fingers, reluctant to take a sip. That was all she needed. Alcohol always made her maudlin and, combined with her current frame of mind, it would be disastrous. Though getting blotto might erase the pain.

'Hi, Kara.'

It was him. Though she couldn't see who spoke close behind her, she knew it with every fibre of her being: the deep voice, the signature aftershave, the heat radiating off him like a roaring bonfire. Her stomach dropped away and her pulse raced. Why was it that even now, after all they had been through, she still responded to him in such a visceral way?

She turned, schooling her face into what she hoped was a cool mask. 'Hello. What are you doing here?'

A small part of her hoped he'd say 'looking for you'. He didn't, and stupidly she was devastated all over again.

'Sally asked me to help out. She needed some shots done for the award.'

He looked amazing in his tux. Why couldn't he look drab for once in his life? It would make it easier to hate him. She knew hate was too strong; maybe not love him as much?

'I'm surprised you came.'

He raised an eyebrow and it lent a rakish quality to his handsome face. 'Why?'

She shrugged, feigning a nonchalance she didn't feel. 'We didn't exactly part on the best of terms yesterday. I thought you wouldn't want to be seen dead with me.'

'That's not right. In fact, it couldn't be further from the truth.'

He took a step closer and their arms brushed, the

impersonal touch sending her body into overdrive. All she could do was stare at him as he continued.

'I needed to see you. To set the record straight.'

Her heart thudded painfully. This was it. He would thank her for being a good friend, for the 'good times' they had shared, and he would walk away. Hell, if she was lucky, he might even offer her the money again, to really rub salt into her open wound.

'There's nothing left to say, Matt. Let's just do this for Sal, OK?' She kept her voice steady when all she felt like doing was crying. It was his fault, looking at her with that look she knew so well, the one he gave her after they made love, all tender and romantic. It hadn't lost its potency one iota. If anything, the thought that they would never share that incredible experience together ever again threatened to set her bawling.

'I think there's plenty to say, but I agree that now probably isn't the best time. How about we go for a stroll after the ceremony and you hear me out?'

'Why should I?' She sounded like a petulant child. She'd never stamped her feet in anger, but right now that was exactly what she felt like doing. However, it wasn't anger that was making her sound irrational. The pain was there, simmering below the surface, dredging up the memories of their time together.

He tipped her chin up and gazed directly into her

eyes, almost as if he was trying to see all the way into her soul. 'Because we owe it to ourselves.'

She shivered in anticipation, yearning to lean forward the last few inches and feel his lips on hers one last time.

'There you two are. Come on, no time for dilly-dallying. They're about to get underway.' Sal appeared out of nowhere, placing an arm around each of them, drawing them towards the open doors.

'I hope you're not up to something?' she whispered in Sal's ear.

'Who? Me?' Sal wore a decidedly sheepish look. 'Never. Hurry up, we'll miss the start.'

The next two hours were the longest of Kara's life. Sal ushered them into their seats, almost shoving her next to Matt. This wouldn't have been so bad if the chairs had been spaced apart like in normal theatres. Instead, in their effort to cram as many people as possible into the room, the organisers had squashed the seats together, bringing her thigh into contact with Matt's muscular one.

Every time he moved an inch she felt it, a shooting sensation of pure pleasure from the area of contact to her core. The more she tried to ignore it, the worse it got, till she almost jumped out of her seat in relief when the presentation ended. Sal's acceptance speech had hardly registered, she'd been so preoccupied with her irrational physical response to the man she'd vowed to forget.

'Time for photos.' He placed a guiding hand under her elbow and led her to the foyer, where the photographer waited. She nodded, not trusting herself to speak and thankful for his supporting hand. Her legs trembled and it had nothing to do with sitting in one seat for too long.

Kara smiled, held Matt's hand and even accepted his kiss on the cheek, all in the name of helping Sal put the finishing touches to her award win and ultimately in saving Matchmaker. Finally, the photographer laid down his camera and they were free to go.

'Thank you, my darlings. You've saved my hide.' Sal enveloped them in a group hug.

Kara stifled a laugh. The older woman couldn't push them together any harder if she tried.

'Now, why don't you two young people run along and have some fun?'

Before she had a chance to respond, Matt stepped in. 'Great idea, Sal. Sure you don't want to join us?'

Sal's grin broadened. 'Wouldn't dream of it. Off you go.' She shooed them towards the door and turned away to greet an acquaintance.

'Well, I guess it's time for that stroll.' He held out his hand to her, that familiar sexy smile doing amazing things to her heartbeat yet again.

Kara had been cautious her whole life. And it had got her nowhere, at least in the love stakes. Caution was for business, for choosing friends, for purchasing cars. Right now, with the man she loved possibly offering her one last fleeting taste of happiness, she decided to throw caution to the wind.

She placed her hand in his, savouring the thrill of his long fingers intertwining with hers. 'I guess it is.'

They walked down the opera-house steps in silence and strolled towards the water's edge. She wondered whether it was the cool night air or the warmth of his touch causing her exposed skin to break out in goosebumps. As if reading her mind, he let go of her hand and slipped out of his jacket.

'Here. Take this.'

He wrapped it around her shoulders, pulling her close.

She inhaled, allowing his intoxicating masculine scent to pervade her senses. God, he smelled good.

'Are you sure? Won't you be cold?'

He slid his hands under the jacket and caressed her upper arms. 'I'm sure. And no, I'm not cold. Now.'

Her heart pounded as he lowered his head. One kiss. Just one. Surely that was allowed? A goodbye kiss she could remember...

As his warm lips touched hers, common sense came flooding back. What was she doing, torturing herself like this? Their deal was finished and the sooner she realised it, the better off she'd be.

'No!' She wrenched her mouth away and stepped back, eager to place as much space between them as possible. She couldn't think when he was that close—her mind turned to mush and her common sense followed suit.

He held her chin and she was forced to look at him. 'You have no idea how I feel, do you?'

She glared at him, tired of the emotional merry-go-round and wanting to jump off right now. Taking a pointed look at his groin area, she replied, 'Oh, I have a fair idea.'

He swore softly and moved away. 'I'm not talking about *that*, though don't think I don't want you right now. I've never stopped wanting you.'

Her shivering increased now that he'd stepped away. For a brief moment, she wished he would hold her again. She folded her arms in a purely defensive gesture. 'What's that supposed to mean?'

'It means I wish I'd never pushed you away all those years ago. It means I wish I hadn't thought up that stupid deal. It means I wish…' He paused, the anguish in his eyes tearing at her.

'Go on,' she urged, hearing his words but not quite believing them.

'I wish that you loved me as much as I love you.'

There, he'd said it. Matt had never thought he

would say those three little words. Now his feelings were finally out in the open. And he hoped to God it wasn't too late.

Her response wasn't predictable. He should have known, for there was nothing predictable about the woman he loved.

'You...you...' She flung herself at him, pounding his chest with her fists.

'Hey! Slow down.' He captured her wrists and held them, staunching the fear in his heart. She hadn't said 'I love you' back, as he'd hoped. Instead, she'd hit him and he didn't have the faintest idea how to respond.

'Say it again,' she whispered, her struggle ceasing.

'Which part?' He couldn't help but tease her. She looked adorable with her strapless dress slipping precariously low, his jacket hanging off one shoulder and her elaborate hairstyle threatening to tumble at any second. Not to mention her wide-eyed look of shock.

'You know. The part about how much you love me.'

A tear slid down her cheek and something inside him broke. It sure wasn't his heart, for that had already shattered the minute he thought he'd lost her.

'I love you. Always have, always will.' He caressed her cheek, sliding his thumb along her jaw line.

'I love you too.' She reached for him, almost frantic to feel his lips against hers.

'No strings? No deals?' he whispered, his lips trailing from her temple to her mouth.

'The only deals you'll be making from now on are in the court room. And don't you forget it!'

Their kiss sealed it.

EPILOGUE

WEDDINGS always made Kara cry. For a business-woman, she could be a real sap and today was no exception.

'Hurry up, darling. We'll be late.' Sal fussed around her, tugging at the satin bustier top encrusted with crystals. 'That's better. It was riding up.'

'A bit like your blood pressure, if you ask me. Relax. You're making me nervous.' As if she wasn't nervous enough for the both of them.

Sal stood back and sniffed. 'You look beautiful. Your folks would've been so proud.'

Kara blinked back tears, knowing the older woman was right. 'Thanks, Sal. For everything.'

Sal dabbed at her eyes. 'Don't thank me. Thank the computer you wanted to blow up not that long ago.'

'I never said I wanted to blow it up! I just thought it'd malfunctioned.'

'Hah! I knew all along that you and Matt were right for each other.' Sal paused, reaching up to kiss her cheek. 'I'm so happy for you.'

'Me too. Though if we don't get a move on, the groom will think I've stood him up.'

Kara almost pinched herself, not quite believing she'd associated the words 'groom' and 'Matt' together. More scary still, today was her wedding day and she was marrying the man of her dreams. Life couldn't get much better than this.

They had chosen to keep it simple, just a handful of friends and family on Matt's yacht. Perfect.

The ride to the harbour passed in a blur as Kara focused on her breathing in a desperate attempt to stay calm.

'Almost there,' the driver announced, pulling the limousine alongside the dock.

'Ready, darling?' Sal reached over and squeezed her hand.

'Ready as I'll ever be.' She reached into the tiny ivory handbag and wrapped her fingers around its contents. This was it.

She practically floated along the wharf, oblivious to the stares, her gaze firmly focused on the striking man in a tux standing on the bow of his yacht.

Matt stepped off the boat and held out his hand. 'You look incredible.'

She swallowed, trying to dislodge the lump of emotion that was stuck in her throat. 'Thanks. So do you.'

'Only the best for my future wife.' He kissed her cheek, lingering for a moment. 'I love you.'

'I love you too, though there's one more thing we need to sort out.'

'What's that?'

She opened her palm and the sunlight glinted off a small metal key. 'You never did tell me what this was all about.'

He smiled, his warmth wrapping her in a familiar embrace. 'Didn't I? Must've slipped my mind.'

'It was a ruse, wasn't it? To get me to go away with you that weekend? You know how I love a challenge.'

'And you know me too well.' His lips brushed hers again. 'Consider it the key to my heart.'

Harlequin Romance®

HIS HEIRESS WIFE

by international bestselling author

Margaret Way

On sale next month in Harlequin Romance

*Welcome to the intensely emotional
world of Margaret Way, where rugged,
brooding bachelors meet their match in the
tropical heat of Australia....*

In *His Heiress Wife* (HR #3811), meet Olivia Linfield,
the beautiful heiress, and Jason Corey, the boy
from the wrong side of the tracks made good.
They should have had the wedding of the decade—
except it never took place. Seven years later Olivia
returns to Queensland to discover Jason installed
as estate manager. Will Jason manage to persuade
the woman he loved and lost how much he still
wants her—and always has...?

*Starting in September,
Harlequin Romance has a fresh new look!
Available wherever Harlequin books are sold.*

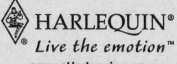

If you enjoyed what you just read,
then we've got an offer you can't resist!

Take 2 bestselling love stories FREE!

Plus get a FREE surprise gift!

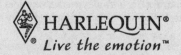

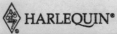

Coming Next Month

#3811 HIS HEIRESS WIFE Margaret Way

Olivia Linfield was the beautiful heiress; Jason Corey was the boy
from the wrong side of the tracks made good. It should have been
the wedding of the decade—except it never took place. Seven years
later Olivia returns to Queensland to discover Jason installed as
estate manager. Should she send him packing…?

The Australians

#3812 THE ENGLISHMAN'S BRIDE Sophie Weston

Sir Philip Hardesty, UN negotiator, is famed for his cool head. But
for the first time in his life this never-ruffled English aristocrat is
getting hot under the collar—over a woman! Kit Romaine, a girl
way below his social class, is not easily impressed. If Philip wants
her, he's going to have to pay!

High Society Brides

#3813 MARRIAGE IN NAME ONLY Barbara McMahon

Wealthy Connor Wolfe has no choice but to marry if he wants to
keep custody of his orphaned niece. Who better as a convenient
wife than his niece's guardian, Jenny Gordon? Jenny agrees—but
secretly she's hoping theirs can be more than a marriage in name
only.…

Contract Brides

#3814 THE HONEYMOON PROPOSAL Hannah Bernard

Joanna has dreamed of marrying Matt from the day they first
kissed—their wedding day, which should have been the happiest
day of her life. But the relationship is a sham, and the marriage
is a fake. So, if it's all pretense, why does it feel so heart-stoppingly
real? And why has Matt proposed a very *real* honeymoon?